False Start

A Second Chance Sports Romance
Ella Haines

LIBRA LIBROS LLC

First edition November 2023

Cover designed by Get Covers

A big thank you to my sensitivity beta readers – Mack, Des, Laurie, Guinevere, and others – thank you for sharing your experiences to make sure this book was the best it could be.

Edited by Imagination Pen Editorial

ISBN 978-1-956865-40-0 (paperback)

ISBN 978-1-956865-41-7 (eBook)

Published by Libra Libros LLC

Contents

Author's Note About Content Warnings   V

Blurb   VI

1. September 25, Sunday   1

2. September 26, Monday   11

3. September 26, Monday   21

4. September 28, Wednesday   27

5. September 29, Wednesday   40

6. September 30, Friday   50

7. October 2, Sunday   59

8. October 5, Wednesday   63

9. October 5, Wednesday Night   69

10. October 6, Thursday   73

11. October 8, Saturday   80

12. October 9, Sunday   91

13. October 10, Monday   98

14. October 10, Monday   105

15. October 11, Tuesday   115

16. October 12, Wednesday   123

17. October 12, Wednesday   129

18. October 12, Wednesday   139

19. October 14, Friday   147

20. October 14, Friday   155

21. October 14, Friday   166

22. October 14, Friday   177

23. October 14, Friday   182

24. Epilogue: October 13, Friday   186

25. Epilogue: October 13, Friday   191

Discover More From Ella Haines   195

Social Media Information - Ella Haines   196

About Author - Ella Haines   197

Request For Review   198

Praise For Ella Haines   199

Content/Trigger Warnings (may contain plot spoilers)   200

Author's Note About Content Warnings

See list of content/trigger warnings here on my site at www.EllaHaines.com/Triggers

The list is also found at the end of the book through the table of contents

WARNING: will possibly contain plot spoilers by nature of disclosing – proceed as you are comfortable

Blurb

Two hearts, a decade of secrets, and the second chance they never saw coming.

**

Emma Potter, a bestselling author, thought she could outrun her past. But when a relentless stalker resurfaces, her carefully constructed world crumbles. Determined to protect those she loves, she's reluctant when her ex-husband demands she stay with him until the culprit is caught. Amidst danger, their unwilling reunion rekindles a love story that betrayal and divorce papers couldn't quite smother.

*

Kyle Justice, a pro football player, has resented Emma for years for her unexpected demand for divorce on the biggest night of his life. Their unexpected reunion triggers a wave of tension, anger, betrayal, and passion in him that proves impossible to ignore. But an unexpected threat thrusts them reluctantly together again. As they navigate treacherous waters, secrets surface, threatening to tear them apart.

*

Emma and Kyle are forced into a race against time, battling unseen enemies and unraveling mysteries that could shatter them. Will they choose to surrender to their past wounds or fight for a future together?

CHAPTER ONE

September 25, Sunday
Emma

Where was he?

The stadium pulsed with infectious energy, a sea of colors and cheers. Sunlight and chants bounced through the stands as fans waved banners and shook cowbells. The smoky aroma of grilling meat wafted through the crisp fall air.

Emma's heart raced, and it wasn't simply due to the excitement in the stands where she was surrounded by her overenthusiastic friends.

"Come on, Ems! Get into it!" Lexie shouted, waving a foam finger in Emma's face. They could have gone into the family booth or owner's box as her dad owned the whole freaking team, but Lexie thrived on the wildness of the crowd. Naturally.

"Can you believe this atmosphere?" Julie shouted over the vuvuzela horns and chants, her eyes wide with excitement.

"Yeah, it's incredible." Emma gave a weak smile.

Why did she think she was ready for this?

Out on the field, the players streamed from the locker room, navy and maroon helmets glinting in the sun.

There he was – number thirty, Kyle Justice, all-star fullback – the love of her life.

Emma's throat tightened at the sight of his muscular frame going through his standard pregame ritual. High knees, butt kicks, run up and jump to touch the goal post.

He hadn't changed his routine at all since high school. However, something about him seemed different. The same could be said about her.

Emma winced as Lexie elbowed her in the ribs and asked, "You're awfully quiet. What's up?"

"Oh, nothing. Just taking it all in."

If she could die without ever admitting to breaking the heart of the one and only Kyle Justice, then she'd be one happy woman. Her friends, no matter how fantastic, would never understand.

"Emma, I can't believe it took this long for you to join us for a game!" Lexie teased, nudging her playfully. "We've been trying to get you here for years!"

"Seriously," Rose chimed in. "We thought we'd have to kidnap you and drag you here."

Laughter bubbled around her, but Emma's smile wavered, the weight of her past looming over her like a shadow.

"Guys, give her a break," Julie interjected, sensing her discomfort. "She's here now, isn't she?"

"True," Lexie conceded, grinning at Emma. "But we all know there's more to this story than just being busy with work."

"Can't a girl focus on her career?" Emma deflected, hoping to steer the conversation away from her past and how the Springfield Spartan's fullback fit into it. Her eyes flickered back to the field, searching for any semblance of an anchor to help ground her in the present moment.

"Of course," Chloe reassured her, patting her on the back. "But—"

"All right," Lexie declared, waving her hands dismissively, "it's kickoff time!"

Her first kickoff in almost a decade.

As the game commenced in a blur of bone-crunching tackles and cleat-churned turf, Emma found her gaze drawn again and again to number thirty.

Old habits die hard.

Then again, there was nothing in the entire stadium that she could look at that didn't provide more pain than comfort...nothing she could look at that wouldn't remind her of the life she gave up.

The set of Kyle's shoulders, the coiled power in his legs as he charged downfield...he was incredible.

Still.

There was an edge to him that hadn't been there before; a darkness that clouded his eyes and a hard set to his jaw whenever the jumbotron showed him up close. His aura had shifted, revealing an intensity that seemed palpable even from the distance of the stands.

Her chest tightened; it was difficult to see such darkness on the face of the man who used to share such easy smiles with her.

Had fame done this to him? Or had she?

As Emma watched Kyle dart between defenders, his powerful strides showcasing his athleticism, she couldn't help the small smile that graced her lips. He did it.

He got his dream.

And that was enough for her.

The game's intricacies came back quickly; she'd spent hours learning the ins and outs of football during their time together. It was a testament to the sheer number of games she had attended that she could still follow each play, especially after all she had been through since then.

"They're absolutely killin' it out there," Chloe gushed, clapping excitedly as the Spartans barreled forward for another first down. Given that her husband was one of the team's tight ends...she was clearly biased, but she wasn't wrong.

"Totally," Emma murmured, her eyes never leaving Kyle.

She felt nostalgic, sad, and brokenhearted, but at the same time proud of what he had achieved. She wished she could have been there for it all, but he never could have reached his dream with her weighing him down.

As the game continued, Emma struggled to focus on her friends' laughter and conversation, with her eyes glued to Kyle, drinking in the familiar sight of him.

He still felt like home to her heart, even after all this time.

A storm of emotions churned within her, each wave crashing against the shore of her conscience.

Did she do the right thing, all those years ago? Where might they be, if she'd chosen a different path?

Emma jumped when a whistle blasted, signaling halftime. The teams gathered themselves and began to jog off the field.

Kyle had achieved everything he ever wanted. She should feel only happiness for him. Instead, regret and longing squeezed her heart.

If only things had been different...

She studied him as he loped off the field. When he passed in front of their section of the sideline, Kyle looked up towards the stands in passing interest at the rambunctious crowd.

And through the blurred chaos of a thousand screaming fans, his eyes locked onto hers.

The chatter and cheers of her friends faded away.

Time froze.

He stuttered to a stop and simply stared. His face was a mixture of shock and anger, a complex swirl of raw emotion momentarily breaking through his stoic resolve.

Emma's breath caught in her throat, pinned by the intensity of his gaze. The years fell away, and she was a young, optimistic girl again, basking in his love.

One of the girls bumped into her arm, causing her to quickly stabilize herself so she didn't topple over. The pull of his stare was magnetic, but she was haunted by the disbelief in his eyes, as he watched her and her companions.

It certainly didn't feel like a decade had passed. The hurt showing in his face certainly still looked fresh.

Her friends continued to chatter, oblivious to the collision of past and present.

A teammate bumped into Kyle, not expecting his abrupt halt while leaving the field. The movement jarred Kyle back to awareness and he blinked quickly as he sucked in a deep breath that had his chest expanding. With one lost look at her, like he couldn't fathom why she would be there, haunting him, he whipped around and jogged after his teammates who were retreating into the Spartan tunnel. His steps were so forceful, Emma imagined she could hear each pounding footfall.

Released from his spell, Emma sagged back against her seat, pulse racing.

Her stomach twisted. This had been a mistake. She wasn't ready to confront the past. Not yet.

Maybe not ever.

"You okay?" Chloe nudged her, voice tinged with concern. "You look like you've seen a ghost."

Emma blinked rapidly. "I'm fine," she said with a shaky laugh. Just spaced out for a minute."

Her friends resumed their lively debate about who was going up to the main concourse to get food and drinks for everyone. She heard them argue about who had to go wait in line, but Emma's chaotic thoughts drowned them out.

She couldn't stop thinking of Kyle's burning gaze. Her heart raced, and she hoped her friends didn't notice the way her hands trembled in her lap.

After several of the girls slipped away to grab their snacks, Lexie scooted closer, still amped about the game. "Did you see that last play? Ryan weighted that throw to Danny perfectly." Lexie squealed.

"Perfectly," Emma repeated, her voice barely a whisper.

"You okay?" Chloe asked, head tilted tenderly. She placed a hand on Emma's shoulder, clearly worried that the massive amount of people and noise was overwhelming her introverted friend.

"Yep," Emma lied, forcing a smile onto her face. "This is just a lot. Haven't been to a game in a while." She didn't want to tell her friends about her history with Kyle or what had caused their breakup. The last thing she needed was for their well-meaning meddling to stir up even more trouble.

The question of whether she had made the right decision years ago played on repeat in her mind, refusing to be silenced. She could feel the pain of their separation as if it were a fresh wound.

The fact that he still seemed to hate her...ouch.

Soon enough, the others came back with armfuls of food.

"Finally! Thank the goddess. I'm starving," Lexie declared, as the tantalizing aroma of stadium food washed over them. "Can someone pass me a hot dog?"

"Here you go," Rose said, handing one over before turning to Emma. She gestured to her wares. "Want something?"

Emma hesitated, her eyes flicking between the greasy foods.

Did her body even *know* how to digest a hot dog anymore? Given the way her stomach churned at the thought of anything heavy or unhealthy...probably not.

"No, thanks," she murmured, uncapping her water instead. "Not really hungry."

Maybe they'd have a healthier option up at one of the kiosks she could get, after the half-time rush calmed down. Besides, her belly was still a ball of nerves.

"Suit yourself," Rose shrugged, biting into a loaded nacho with gusto.

"Oh! Emma, did you manage to send that manuscript off to the publisher last night?" Julie asked before taking a bite of pretzel.

"Uh, yeah, I got it off just in time." Emma forced herself to tune back into the conversation around her, pushing thoughts of Kyle from her mind.

"Amazing," Julie praised, giving her a supportive wink. "You go, girl."

"Thanks," Emma said, her voice barely audible.

"By the way, congratulations on your latest book release," Chloe chimed in, giving her a light nudge on the shoulder. "I heard it sold out of the local bookstores within hours. You're releasing super-fast this year!"

"Thanks. I stockpiled a few for a rapid release strategy for my indie readers," Emma replied, her cheeks flushing with a mix of pride and embarrassment. Writing had always been her refuge, but she never expected to find such success in it.

But Kyle had encouraged her...

"Oh, and I also forgot to tell you. We got the new rescue foals in," gushed Julie. As owner of the nonprofit Foals & Fillies, Julie knew Emma had a soft spot for animals. Emma frequently volunteered on weekends, grateful for the peace working with the horses brought her. "They're absolutely precious," Julie continued. "You'll have to come out tomorrow to meet them. It'll be good therapy time, too."

Emma managed a real smile at that. Julie was one of the few who knew about her health battle over the years – ones that had left Emma withdrawn and struggling to adjust to her new normal. Time with the horses helped ground her and put her life back into perspective.

"I'll be there," Emma promised.

A roar went up from the crowd as the teams made their way back out onto the field. With halftime ending, the fans' beers and bellies had been refilled and the energy level was higher than ever.

Emma avoided looking at Kyle. She focused instead on the refreshing breeze, the energy of the fans around her, the warmth of the sun on her face. For now, she just wanted to enjoy this day with her friends; she could curl up and cry about what might have been later tonight when she got home.

However, no matter how much she tried to ignore it, the guilt still gnawed at her.

She had walked away from their marriage without explanation, determined to free him from the drama of her life. It was the only way he could achieve his dreams.

Or so she had thought at the time.

Now, seeing the bitterness in his eyes, she wondered if she'd made the right choice.

She focused on the field, the players, and the game itself – anything to keep from dwelling on the painful memories she'd buried for so long. As the autumn wind played with her hair, she couldn't help but wonder when she would finally feel like she moved on.

It was half of the reason she agreed to come today, finally, after all these years.

She wanted to see if she could do it without wanting to cry.

She couldn't.

Now that the Spartans were on offense, she felt safe looking back down to the field. There was no way Kyle would be making angry eye contact with her now.

Emma tried to focus on the game, but her attention kept drifting to Kyle on the sidelines. Did he carry the same scars from their relationship that she did?

Maybe some doors were better left closed. She'd coped these last few years by locking away the past.

So why was she here? Reopening those wounds like an idiot?

She had to keep moving forward.

The past was done, but the future was hers to shape. She would focus on the joys in front of her – her work, her friends, and the horses who never failed to lift her spirits. One step at a time, she would form the life she wanted. The life she deserved. Even if it was without the love of her life...the man she had loved with all her heart.

The man she had forced to the sidelines of her life.

The man standing on the sidelines in front of her.

The final drive of the game played out in a whirlwind of frenetic energy, with players giving their all. Emma's heart raced, mirroring the chaotic atmosphere that enveloped the stadium. Her eyes remained locked on Kyle's back.

Was this the last time she'd see him?

She couldn't decide how she felt about that.

When the giant timer on the jumbotron ran out, the crowd exploded into cheers. Emma's friends celebrated and hugged each other, swept up in the euphoria of the Spartan's victory.

But Emma felt nothing.

"Next time we should get tickets closer to the field! Maybe we can get some autographs," Chloe joked with a wink and a grin, her eyes gleaming with amusement.

"Loser," Lexie chuckled back.

Emma managed a small smile at her joke, but it fell away as her gaze drifted back towards the field where Kyle still stood.

"I don't think there'll be a next time for me," she admitted, quietly.

No good could come from seeing him again; it was best to keep her distance.

"Really? But we had so much fun!" Rose protested, her brow furrowing in concern. "You sure you're okay, Em?"

"Of course," Emma lied, offering her friends a reassuring smile. "It's just...not really my scene, you know?"

"All right," Lexie's ice blue eyes narrowed with suspicion, but she surprisingly chose not to press matters further. "If you change your mind, you know we'll be here. Being an owner, it's my duty to come and cheer on the team. You always have a seat with me."

Emma gave a soft nod of thanks.

As they grabbed their things to escape up to the VIP lounges, Emma sighed and looked once more out at the players mingling on the field, celebrating and giving interviews.

"Let's head out," Lexie commanded, leading the way.

As they filed out of their seats, Emma cast one last glance at the field. The crackling possibilities of what might have been still called to her, but she turned away. The past was done.

Yet all these years and still, one look from Kyle still had the power to unravel her.

Maybe she wasn't as put together as she pretended to be. She clearly wasn't ready to see him again. She'd fought so hard to reclaim her life once already, she didn't want to have to do it again.

With a heavy heart, Emma followed her friends through the various doors and stairwells, each step taking her further from the past she so desperately wanted to forget. With a deep breath, she pushed the thoughts away. The past was best left there. It was time to close this door for good. She would move forward, not backward.

And keep the memories where they belonged – in the shadows of what might have been.

CHAPTER TWO

September 26, Monday
Emma

Emma sat alone at a table in Victor's Diner, her eyes scanning the pages in front of her as she scribbled down her thoughts and marked edits on her manuscript. The pounding rain slashed on the window next to her in her booth and acted as a great white noise when combined with the quiet hum of the restaurant's patronage. She plopped her elbow on the table at a right angle, and then dumped her chin in her palm.

Schnikes, she *really* hated editing.

She struggled to stay focused on the manuscript in front of her. She had finished this rough draft a few months ago but had to table it for a higher priority manuscript that her publisher was asking for. Now that the other manuscript was done and out of her hands, she needed to buckle down and finally revisit this one.

It was crap.

She was crap.

How could people read her work and not cringe?

Gah! Imposter syndrome was hitting her hard.

She tucked a strawberry blonde wisp back behind her ear, even though she knew it was just going to slip out and tickle her cheek again.

As irritating as it could be, she couldn't bring herself to cut it.

Her friends were laughing in a corner booth, and she was more than willing to distract herself and look up in passing curiosity.

Anything other than looking at this flaming pile of dog poo manuscript in front of her. Did she even know there were other forms of punctuation besides an exclamation point?

Chloe caught her eyes and waved her over. Emma shook her hand and mouthed 'not today.'

Duty, no matter how frustrating, was calling..

Just then, as she turned to buckle down on her work, the universe seemed to try to test her dedication. The door to the diner creaked open, and in walked the breaker of souls, himself.

Kyle.

Her heart stuttered.

His dark hair was damp and stuck to his forehead. His deep eyes scanned the room for an empty seat and Emma tensed, sliding down in the booth the slightest bit.

Don't see me, don't see me, don't see me.

She'd been in this city for five freaking years, and she'd never bumped into him!

Now, twice in two days?

She never should have gone to that stupid game.

Pandora's Box, anyone? It was like she was freaking asking the universe for trouble.

"Of all the diners in Springfield," she muttered under her breath, "he had to walk into this one."

Almost like he heard her, Kyle's gaze locked onto her, and her heart stopped.

Shoot.

Kyle stood frozen, watching her. She saw the moment his shock shifted to stubborn resolve. That familiar clench of his jaw, the tension in his broad shoulders. He'd never been one to back down from a challenge.

Emma's heart raced as he stalked towards her table, boots thudding heavily on the tile floor, leaving wet tracks on the linoleum. She fidgeted with her pen, unsure what to say after so many years apart. Their gazes were locked, blue on brown, both wary and untrusting.

Kyle cleared his throat gruffly as he stopped by Emma's table, his imposing frame casting a shadow over her notebook. "Emma," Kyle's voice was strained as he loomed over her. "What the hell are you doing here?"

Her heart skipped a beat as memories of stolen kisses and whispered promises flooded back. She quickly looked away, cheeks burning with a mix of embarrassment and horror.

God was absolutely a sadist.

"I'm working." Her voice squeaked out higher than she intended.

Real smooth.

"In my city?" He ground out, his tooth enamel chipping away with each word.

"I live here; I have for years." She couldn't help but wince at the sharpness of his words, his impressive, dark scowl causing a painful twinge in her chest.

"Bullshit." He spat the word out. "What do you want?"

"I don't want anything, Kyle." She leveled him with a look. "I'm serious. I moved to Springfield at least a year before you were traded, so don't take that attitude with me. I did nothing to deserve it."

His dark eyebrows shot up and he reared back like she slapped him.

"Nothing to deserve it? Are you high?"

Emma flinched.

"You're saying it was just a coincidence that I've seen you twice in two days when you've supposedly been here for years?" His hands saddled on his hips as he snarked, "Yeah, right. So, cut the shit. What do you want?"

"Yes, chance encounters do exist. I come here all the time, just ask Victor." She tossed her head towards where the owner was watching them from behind the counter. Emma wet her lips and tried to give him a peace offering. "But I will admit that it was a bad choice to attend a game. I didn't...I didn't expect you to see me. I'm sorry about that. I didn't think it through."

"Clearly. It was heartless and thoughtless of you to go. What kind of game are you trying to play? Haven't you done enough?" Kyle berated.

Emma fidgeted with her pen. "No game. Like I said, I'm sorry. And don't worry. It wasn't fun for me either. I won't be going back again—"

"Oh, I know you won't be going back again. I'm going to be talking to security as soon as I leave here."

She furrowed her brows at him. "Come on, Kyle. I already said I regretted going and that I'm sorry that I put you in that position. I didn't think of the consequences. I already said I won't go back. Move on."

Wrong choice of words.

He slammed a fist on the table and the clatter of her silverware made her jump.

"Oh, don't worry. I did. I fucking *moved on* all over this *fucking country*. I am the *very definition* of 'moved on.'" His voice was a grumbly hiss. She didn't know that was possible, but here he was, doing a grumbly hiss. "And I'm going to stay that way. And I don't need whatever drama you're planning to enter into my stratosphere. So, if you'd be so kind, please leave and bring whatever shit you have swirling around with you."

This was the man she'd once loved with every fiber of her being, the man who had always been so protective and shielding, and now this is how they were.

Emma bit back a sharp retort. Arguing would get them nowhere.

"Can we talk about this? Calmly?"

As an incensed expression came over his face, a noise from the girls' table had them both turning their heads to look at them, saving Emma from an imminent tongue lashing.

All the eavesdroppers looked away quickly, suddenly interested in the architecture of the ceiling and design of the table mats.

Except Lexie.

Who now stared at Kyle with a raging expression on her face, her eyes narrowed on his looming posture over Emma.

Out of respect for his team's owner's daughter, Kyle shifted away from Emma. Barely. And he looked back at Emma.

Kyle's eyes narrowed. "They're off limits too. Don't go poisoning them against me."

Emma flushed. "I would never—"

"Just stay away, Emma," Kyle growled. "I don't want you in my life. Stay away from my city, my home, my diner, my *friends*. You've caused enough damage."

"They're my friends too," Emma snapped. "And I was here first!"

It was incredible how well they knew each other's tics even after all this time. The way his eyes traced the movement of her fingers as she tucked that stupid loose strand of hair behind her ear; the way she knew that after barking at her like that, he would likely clench his fists, trying to contain the raging storm inside him.

They glared at each other, tension crackling. His eyes dropped to her hands, watching her twist the pen between her fingers.

A long-time nervous habit.

Emma's traitorous gaze traced the rain-soaked edge of his shirt, clinging to broad shoulders.

A subtle cough interrupted the stare-down. Their heads swiveled to see Victor standing here, glaring at Kyle like he was caught with his hand in the candy jar. "I like you, boy. You and your teammates are like my long-lost nephews. But I don't like you harassing my girls. You might be a nephew, but she's a *daughter*. Take off and go cool down. Probably about time for you to leave." The old man's grouchy and war-torn eyes stared hard at Kyle.

Kyle stiffened and stared at the older man in anger, disbelief, and betrayal.

Victor continued in his gruff voice. "Like I said, I like you, and I have no idea what you two have going on right now. But you're making a scene in my diner, and I'm not overly fond of the words and way you're hovering over her. Ya hear?"

Kyle took a step back in insult. "I wasn't going to hit her!" His face was appalled at the thought. His eyes darted to Emma, and he stilled, his face slackening for a minute as he took in her tight posture that was leaning away from him, and the white, clammy sheen on her face.

"Shit. Emma. I—"

"Like, I said, son. Probably time for you to leave."

With one last confused, hurt, and angry glance at Emma, Kyle left, with the diner door slamming behind him. The bell's ding echoed around the roaring in her head.

How no one was staring at her, and gaping was a testament to the iron fist that Victor ruled with. People didn't come to his diner to gawk at the local celebrities and get in their business.

Except for the girls in the corner.

Shit.

Emma slumped back in her seat, unable to get control of her feelings. After she was certain the tears weren't going to fall, she looked up at Victor. "Thanks for looking out for me, but you didn't need to. Kyle wouldn't have hurt me. Ever."

And any hurtful words he did voice came from a place of pain that *she* gave him. She deserved it all. It was her penance.

"Lots of ways to hurt someone, kid." With a nod, the old veteran turned and stomped back to the kitchen.

Ignoring the chattering of her friends clearly talking about her, she picked up her pen with a shaky hand. Emma bent her head and tried to focus on work again, but her mind was too scattered to form any coherent thoughts.

Her pen hovered over the page uselessly.

Come on, girl. Focus!

With a determined huff, Emma forced her red pen down onto the page.

There, she'd missed a comma.

There, she had one where it wasn't needed at all.

This was where her attention belonged – on the pages before her, not on the man who'd once held her heart.

Maybe she'd write him into a story. He'd be the perfect hero. Tall, dark, handsome, brooding, alpha, fiercely protective. Perfect.

And then she could kill him.

But her heart squeezed at the thought.

No. No, she'd never be able to kill the essence of him, even in a novel.

As angry and as hurt as she was right then...he was more so.

And he was justified.

She broke his heart without warning.

And because of that, she deserved every inch of hate he threw her way.

Emma pinched her lips together and set her pen down. She rubbed at her temples and tried not to break out into tears.

All she could do was try to move forward, one step at a time, and hope that eventually, the pain would fade away.

As she started back in on her edits, the image of Kyle's stormy eyes and clenched fists haunted her. Despite everything, she couldn't resist the undeniable pull she still felt toward him. She closed her eyes, trying to shut out the memories of his touch and the taste of his lips.

She glanced up as the whispers from her friends' table grew louder. They weren't even trying to pretend they weren't gossiping about her and Kyle.

Emma knew these women all too well; they were relentless in their pursuit of information and even more so when it came to matchmaking. Their involvement was the last thing she needed right now, but there was no escaping the fact that they'd seen everything.

She needed to come clean about their marriage and divorce or the girls would be meddling and causing more hurt to Kyle.

He didn't deserve that.

With a sigh, Emma packed up her stuff. There would be no more editing today. At least not here in the diner.

Emma took a deep breath and walked over to her friends' table.

Her friends leaned forward eagerly, concerned questions swirling in their eyes.

"Girl," Rose crooned with a teasing glint in her eyes. "You got some 'splainin' to do. It's not every day that our quiet little author finds herself tangled up in a steamy sports romance of her own. What's up with you and our-boy-smolder? You failed to mention any history there, yesterday at the game." Her red eyebrows were arched delicately as she waited for an answer.

Ugh, she knew this was going to happen.

Before the others could join in on the attack, Emma held up a hand. "I know you're dying of curiosity. But it's a long story, and I'm not ready to get into it yet. If ever. Let's just say we were young and stupid, once. Got married, then divorced just as quickly."

Emma gave a rueful laugh, trying to imply it wasn't something huge.

Something life changing.

Something *real*.

Because it was. It was so real and true and magical, that here she was, years later, still broken from it.

But their divorce had been for the best. It was the only reason that Kyle was able to be where he was today.

"What?" Lexie exclaimed, her ice blue eyes wide.

"Are you sure you're okay?" Chloe asked, exchanging concerned glances with the others. "You know you can talk to us, right?"

"Yeah," Emma murmured, forcing a smile. "I know."

The girls exchanged glances, clearly reluctant to let it go.

"Well, we're here when you want to talk." Megan said, twisting her lips into a small smile. "We all have our secrets that we'll share when we're ready. If ever."

Emma nodded, gratitude welling up. She gave them a soft smile of thanks and turned to go, even as the echo of Kyle's hurt words still reverberated in her ears.

Her heart ached, that familiar pain she'd tried so hard to bury resurfacing, again.

She had loved him with every fiber of her being.

When he was gone…so was her world.

She said her goodbyes as she left the diner on autopilot. She gave a wry smile of apology to a woman sitting across the way who was staring at her in horror at the scene that had just transpired in such a public place. Emma burned under the judgmental green eyes of the strange woman. Judgmental Judy must not have gotten the memo to pretend not to witness her and Kyle's…confrontation.

In her mind, Emma saw Kyle's face when she'd told him she wanted a divorce, right before the NFL draft. Bad timing, but she'd had her reasons – she'd only been trying to protect him and not spoil his night. But the shock and betrayal in his eyes still haunted her nightmares. He hadn't understood. How could he? She couldn't tell him the truth without stripping him of his dreams.

Leaving Kyle had been the hardest thing she'd ever done. But it had been for his own good.

Emma hustled out the door into the pouring rain and let the droplets momentarily join the tears rushing down her cheeks. She took a shaky breath and set her jaw in determination.

Tackle today.

It was something Kyle's coaches had drilled into him growing up, and he'd passed it on to her. When they got married right out of high school and faced ridicule from their small town, he'd repeated those words to her, offering comfort and encouragement. Now she whispered it to herself in Kyle's absence.

She didn't know what tomorrow would bring but she would tackle today.

And maybe one day, she could finally find peace in the choices she had made.

CHAPTER THREE

September 26, Monday
Kyle

Kyle stomped out of the diner, ignoring the rain that soaked through his clothes and caused his skin to prickle at the chill.

In fact, bring it on. It mirrored the storm of emotions churning inside – fury, confusion, resentment.

And a little bit of guilt for snapping at Emma. But only just a little bit; she did destroy their marriage and upend his life, after all.

He blew out a breath. Emma was *here*. In his town, in his diner, hanging out with his friends.

How dare she just show up, back into his life, like nothing happened?

He stormed through the security gate at the Spartans' complex, marching his way across the parking lot. He'd tell them to blacklist her later, when he could form a coherent sentence.

And now his stomach growled in protest, adding insult to injury.

The selfish witch had made him abandon his meal.

Why was she even prettier now? With those stupid, adorable glasses – which were ridiculous, because she always had perfect eyesight.

Also, what was up with the long hair?

She used to wear it short, thick and straight. Now it was curly, and all sun-strawberry perfection. What the fuck?

The Emma he knew would never have taken the time to do her hair every day.

He ground his teeth. The Emma he knew was gone.

Except she wasn't, not literally at least.

Why was she here?

Had she come to flaunt her new look? Her success? Rub her life in his face?

He kicked an empty can on the ground.

First, she rips his heart out, only hours before the biggest night of his life.

Then, she has the audacity to miraculously show up again, invading his domain?

The wound tore open again, raw and aching.

Well, fuck that shit. Kyle wasn't going to let her turn his world upside down again.

No way. No matter what she was trying to pull.

Kyle slammed into the locker room, water dripping from his hair. The few teammates standing around looked up in surprise.

"Whoa, what happened to you?" Michael asked.

"Go for an unexpected swim?" Kenny joined in with a smile.

Kyle scowled and flipped them off. "I ran into an evil succubus who's apparently stalking me."

The others exchanged amused glances, though Liam at least looked concerned.

Well, at least someone was taking this seriously.

"A stalker, huh?" John said from the corner. Ryan, their young quarterback, sat next to John, icing his shoulder.

"I saw her at the game yesterday with the girls. Then, she showed up at Victor's today just to fuck with me. It's like she's infiltrating every part of my life on purpose."

Kenny raised a disbelieving eyebrow. "Emma? You're talking about Emma?" His voice went high in the end.

Kyle froze and the roaring in his head turned quiet. He stilled his movement toward his locker and swiveled his head to Kenny. "Wait...how do you know her?"

Actually, all the men were looking at him like he was nuts.

Liam gave him a puzzled expression. "We all know Emma. She's wicked nice. She hangs out with the girls. They're all in a book club together." Liam frowned at Kyle. "I mean, they hang out together all the time. Surely you've seen her around before now…"

Kyle bristled. Nice? Emma had ripped his still-beating heart from his chest and smashed it to pieces. There was nothing nice about her.

And what's this about 'all the time?'

"Well, you don't know her like I do, apparently," he grumbled. "And no, I've not 'seen her around.'" He spat the words out.

Kenny clapped him on the back. "Chin up, man. Don't let her get to you, I'm sure whatever shit that happened between you wasn't on purpose. Like Liam said, she's a sweetheart."

The others murmured in agreement.

Fucking fuckers! They were clueless.

Kyle squeezed his fists tight so as not to punch a hole in the wall closest to him.

"Yeah, tell that to my divorce certificate on the desk at home. She's a real harmless piece of work." He snarled at them all and stomped to the bag he left in the corner.

Surely he had some extra clothes in there.

He ripped the items out in clumps, not registering what he was pulling out.

One thing was certain – he wouldn't let Emma disrupt his life again. This time he'd stay two steps ahead. No fucking way he'd let her get close enough to wreak such devastation again.

Ryan's incredulous voice cut through the locker room banter and the clatter of his things being rifled through. "Wait, divorce certificate?" The younger man paused when he noticed Kyle freeze. "You were married? To Emma?"

What was Golden Boy's deal with Emma?

Kyle slowly turned around and pinned the young quarterback with a dark squint. "What of it?"

"I just...can't believe you married someone as sweet and even-tempered as her," Ryan continued, shaking his head in disbelief.

Kyle stiffened further. What the fuck did that mean?

Ryan went on, extolling Emma's gentle nature, her quiet strength, her creativity.

Were they fucking sleeping together? What the fuck.

With each new word of praise, Kyle had to fight the growing urge to punch Ryan right in the throat as his own jealousy and bitter resentment bubbled.

Emma had betrayed their love. She didn't deserve Ryan's admiration – or anyone else's, for that matter.

Sensing the fury raging in Kyle, Ryan backtracked. "Hey man, I don't know what happened but maybe she's changed. She's really sweet. Like a true to her core, sweet. Like Chloe. So, I don't know how she used to be, but that's not who she is anymore." He held up his hands in a calming gesture and glanced around at the other men for affirmation.

The traitors all nodded along, happy to choose her side.

Fuckers.

Kyle nodded tightly, jaw clenched.

Their eyes were heavy on him, no doubt wondering what the hell had happened between him and Emma.

No doubt they'd get a similar recounting from their ladies when they got home that night.

Then they'd all get caught up into thinking this was some little drama that could be fixed with a hug and a kiss.

They would think that despite everything, Emma still had an emotional hold over him, so that must mean he still cared. So therefore, they'd meddle.

Mistakenly.

She had no hold over him. Not anymore. And he didn't want to care.

No – he didn't care.

Kyle bristled under the scrutiny of his teammates' gazes. Their raised eyebrows spoke volumes.

They had no idea of the true depths of her betrayal; one that he'd equate to kicking a dog. Unforgivable.

Kyle opened his mouth to lobby his side, but quickly shut it again. He didn't owe them details.

Instead, he took a deep, calming breath and tried to let the tension out of his fists. "It's not what you think," he muttered. "We're through for good." He grabbed a towel from his pile of shit and wiped vigorously at his damp face and sopping hair.

A few teammates nodded, but most still wore infuriating all-knowing expressions. They didn't believe him.

Kyle ground his teeth in frustration.

Emma had them all fooled. Sure, Emma had fooled him once with her sweet façade, too – but never again.

Fuck, he was going to explode.

Kyle peeled off his rain-soaked shirt, and loosely toweled off his chest while his thoughts bitterly churned.

His stomach growled again.

Fucking fucker.

Sure, he could just order a sandwich from the cafeteria, but he'd wanted Victor's famous veggie club sandwich. And now apparently he could never go back, not without possibly running into *her.*

It was just one more comfort she had stolen from him.

Emma.

Why was she here? What was her angle?

Kyle jerked on a dry t-shirt, then shorts, before slinging his wet clothes on some hooks by his locker.

Did she want money?

His fists clenched at the idea.

That had to be it. Why else would she show up now, acting like everything was fine? Tricking everyone into believing she was a guiltless party in his heartache?

Kyle's jaw tightened. Well, he wouldn't give her the satisfaction of seeing him rattled. Next time he saw her, he'd be ready. He'd get confirmation about why she was here, then send her packing.

He ripped out his phone and shot off a text to Chloe – she might not get back to him for a couple of days because of work and her two girls, but that was fine. It was worth the wait. If he asked anyone else, they'd be up in his face in a heartbeat. Chloe was the most likely to respond and the least likely to pry. Ryan wasn't wrong – Chloe was good people. Like he used to think Emma was.

As soon as he got Emma's address, he'd go snooping. See how long she had lived there, what it looked like, if it was ugly or run down...which he sort of hoped it would be, because that's what Emma deserved.

However, until he got her address, he needed to focus on football. Emma had already derailed his career once. He wouldn't let it happen again. Grabbing his tablet, Kyle headed to an empty classroom, his expression set in grim determination.

Tackle today.

He'd been fooled by her act once before. Never again. This time he was ready for her games. She'd get nothing from him.

Except a one-way ticket out of his life.

Chapter Four

September 28, Wednesday
Emma

Emma pulled into her little driveway and let out a soft sigh. She was having a crap few days after making that stupid decision to go to that stupid game.

Stupid!

Then, running into Kyle in person?

Gah!

The entire week was becoming a train wreck. She just couldn't focus.

Maybe a mid-week break was what she needed to get things back on track.

So, instead of hunkering down at her computer, Emma ran away and spent the day cuddling ponies.

Well, not technically 'ponies.' They were *horses*. Though Julie did stable some ponies there...

But saying 'pony' in her head felt cozier.

She grabbed her bag, slid out of the car and jogged up to her front door. In the distance, she could see the Woodland Park Conservation Area and she made a mental note to go for a quick walk later, given the nice weather.

Fall in New England could change in a heartbeat.

Emma stepped through the front door of her house and stopped dead.

The lingering joy from her day volunteering at Foals and Fillies evaporated instantly.

The living room looked like a tornado had torn through it – furniture overturned, belongings strewn and shattered on the hardwood floors. Her heart clamped with dread, suffocating the contentment she'd felt just moments before.

"What the hell?" she whispered as she took in the destruction: photos knocked off walls, shelves emptied, cushions gutted.

Kicking aside debris, Emma moved cautiously through the wreckage. She couldn't comprehend how this had happened.

Her sanctuary...her home...

A folded piece of paper on the kitchen island caught her eye. Hands trembling, Emma unfolded it, the words scribbled in harsh black letters:

'You don't deserve to be happy. I'll show you what real pain feels like.'

The note fluttered from her fingers. This wasn't just some random act of destruction – someone had deliberately targeted her.

But who?

Why?

She heard a scrape echo down the hallway from the back room and she froze, her heartbeat thumping in her ears.

What was that? Was whoever had done this still in the house?

Better yet – what was she still doing here? As soon as she saw the mess, she should have turned and gone back into her car, locked the doors, and called the cops!

Fear skittered up Emma's spine.

She needed to get out of there. Now.

She turned to flee but as she bolted, her foot caught on an upended stool. She crashed to the floor, banging her forehead on the nearby granite countertop.

"Oof!"

Warm blood trickled down her forehead, but adrenaline propelled her back to her feet.

Get out, get out, get out.

Another small floorboard squeak had her whipping around towards the back hallway.

Oh god, someone was still back there!

Her brain screamed while her feet kicked into overdrive.

Get out, get out, get out.

Bursting through the front door and sprinting towards the road to find help, Emma lamented her weak muscles. A horn blared as a giant vehicle swerved to avoid her as she lurched out of her driveway and into the road. Emma dove out of the way before pausing to catch her breath, glancing between the neighbor's houses, hoping to find someone who was home – but the sound of trailing footsteps had her heart jumping into her throat.

When a large hand snared down onto her shoulder and spun her around, Emma let out a roaring scream.

She thrashed, kicked, and punched, trying to fight the attacker off, screaming all the while.

Strong hands gripped her arms, pulling her close and stilling her movements. Disoriented, she looked up ... into Kyle's handsome face. His eyes were stormy, dark with concern, as they took in the blood dripping down her face and her terrified shaking.

"Emma? What the fuck is going on?"

His voice enveloped her like a security blanket, soothing her frantic heart. She relaxed in his arms and started babbling, trying to explain the chaos inside while Kyle's gaze remained fixed on her intently.

His eyes darted over her head and narrowed as he glared at the front door of her home that was hanging open, ominously.

"I...I...I think the person is still in there. I think I heard something from the back room." Or maybe it was her imagination? "Maybe. I don't know. Maybe I didn't..."

Her jaw was chattering so hard it was difficult to speak clearly.

"Stay close to me, I don't want you out of my sight."

Before she could protest, Kyle pulled her hand into his and dragged her back into the house, keeping her hand in his. Emma stumbled on her trashed belongings as she struggled to keep pace with Kyle as he marched to where she indicated with a shaking finger, where she'd thought she'd heard the noise.

Shouldn't they be calling the police?

She wrote thrillers under a separate pen name, so she knew about police procedurals.

And also, about how it was freaking stupid to go into a house where an assailant could be lurking!

Even so, Kyle's assertive and protective presence eased her panic.

No one would hurt her with him around. Except for maybe him with his words. If that was the case, she deserved it.

She heard him curse loudly and jerk to a halt. He quickly turned and placed his hands on her shoulders, moving her backward into the hall and out of the bedroom doorway where they had stopped.

Heart in her throat, she looked up into his face, where his jaw was clenched, and his eyes flashed.

Oh boy.

"What is it?"

Did she even want to know?

Kyle shook his head and his nostrils flared.

"I need to see." Emma pushed.

Surely, he recognized that...

He must have, because his hands dropped away, but he stood close behind her when she moved to enter the doorway of her bedroom.

Vomit lodged in her throat.

On the center of her bedspread, a quilt made for her by her loving grandmother, one that she and Kyle had cuddled under for years, was a dead cat.

Not just dead...but...mutilated.

She tasted bile as it moved further up her throat.

Dry blood soaked its calico fur and its eyes stared blankly ahead. Forever unseeing. Its fur was matted, and a lone fly swarmed around it.

There was a book sitting under the cat's poor head. *The Coup de Grâce*. Her latest thriller. One that featured a dead cat as a message to the protagonist. Also, next to the thriller, was her latest rom-com, and her latest children's picture book.

All three of her pen names...covered in blood.

Another wave of nausea hit her, and she covered her mouth.

Apparently that was enough for Kyle, because he grabbed her again and steered her from the house and to the driveway, his eyes constantly scanning their surroundings. He clocked a car in a driveway down the road and his head cocked for a moment before returning to his survey of the area.

He steered Emma to his Range Rover that was pulled over haphazardly on the side of the road and loaded her into the passenger seat. He must have pulled over when he saw her running.

"Was that your cat? Do you always leave your bedroom window open? Was your front door unlocked when you got home?" He asked in rapid-fire succession.

"What?" She blinked at him, her brain not working right.

He was staring at his phone in his hand as he continued to scan the street and yards. Kyle placed the phone to his ear and asked again,.

"How did the person get in? Did you notice?"

She shook her head, her entire body shivering with the shock.

A well of hysteria bubbled up in her and she wrapped her arms around her torso, trying to compress her own nervous system.

She couldn't stop the outburst. "Guess the cat's out of the bag and onto the bed."

Jeesh, what was wrong with her?

Kyle slowly turned and stared at her, like she was some alien that just landed on earth.

Crap, she was a mess.

She rolled her lips together and started rocking back and forth, trying to channel the nerves.

Kyle spoke to someone on the other end of the phone, while he cased the block for anything suspicious. When he hung up, he turned to her. "The police will be here shortly. They'll do their thing, ask you some questions, and then we'll get going."

What? Where? Wait…we?

Regardless, her head just bobbed along with what he was saying. It didn't even matter what he said at this point. His voice was grounding her; that was all she needed.

"In the meantime, what can you tell me about this?"

Emma shook her head helplessly. "Na-na-nothing. I mean, I've gotten some weird calls and letters over the years, but nothing like this."

Kyle scowled, raking a hand through his cropped black hair.

"Fuck. Anyone you've pissed off recently?" He paused. "Besides me."

Emma shook her head again. "No - no one."

"I'm serious, Em. Now's not the time to save face. Any jilted exes that are demanding their pound of flesh?"

Hurt sliced through her jitters and her bouncing knees slowed.

"No, Kyle." What more was there to say?

He gave her a disbelieving look, his eyes once again drifting to the curl of her hair, and he snorted.

Gah! How could she want to punch him and have him hold her at the same time?

Instead, she remained mute and tried to settle her rioting nerves. She needed to be coherent when the cops arrived.

The hard part about being an author was that she tended to get chatty and over-explain things. She knew she was doing it but couldn't seem to make herself stop. Who knew what piece of evidence would help catch the cat killer?

With Kyle brooding at her back, she explained to the arriving officers what happened not only that evening, but what happened yesterday, the day before, and the day before that. By the time she was done, the officers knew about her ill-fated attempt to go to a Spartans game and the resulting heartache that followed. They knew what she ate for breakfast, right down to where she bought her organic blueberries. No piece of information was going to be overlooked. Not on her watch.

When it came time for them to ask her about potential suspects, Kyle finally stopped his incessant pacing and hovered, clearly interested in her answer.

"Like I told Kyle earlier, I've had random messages and things sent to me, it's part of the gig. Usually, they're very sweet and supportive. Sometimes they're weird and quirky. Very rarely are they sketchy. My PA does an excellent job of filtering that crap out."

"Exes?"

She could feel Kyle's eyes on her. Well, crap.

"None."

"We're going to need names."

Fine.

"Okay. Kyle Justice."

The officers blinked and looked back up at Kyle before turning back to her. "We need the other names as well. If you feel more comfortable—"

"No, it's fine. That's all there is. Kyle. No one since. We don't need to sneak away from him. I have nothing to hide."

Well...in this case at least.

Something caught their attention over her head and their faces quickly became neutral as they zipped back down to marking up the notepad in front of them.

She was nervous of what they saw in Kyle's face.

What was he thinking?

She refused to look. Some things were better left unknown.

As the officers wrapped up their work on the house, Emma was given the all clear to grab the bare minimum of things before leaving for the night. When she asked the nearest officer for his recommendation for the safest local hotel, Kyle barged in and pulled her away.

"Ignore her. She's in shock. She doesn't need a hotel."

Emma whipped her face up to see him. "What? Of course, I do, Kyle! I can't possibly stay here tonight."

He gave her an impassive look. "I know. You obviously can't stay here alone. At least not until you install a security system. So, pack a bag like you were going to, and then you're coming home with me."

Emma blinked in surprise. After everything between them, she was not expecting that.

"Um, Kyle..."

"Just leave it, Em."

"But—"

"I said, leave it."

She rolled her lips together and nodded slowly.

Common sense prevailed.

Safe was safe. And being with Kyle was even safer.

She wasn't so depressed with her life that she didn't care about her safety. At least, not anymore.

Emma's heart hammered against her ribs as she shoved some clothes and toiletries into a bag with trembling hands.

But the fact that Kyle still felt a sliver of protectiveness...

What did that mean?

If it was anyone else, surely he would have told them to stay at a hotel...right?

Being near him again was stirring up memories – lazy mornings curled in his arms, breathless laughter on nighttime escapades. A wave of longing caught her off guard and she closed her eyes tight.

No. She couldn't go down that rabbit hole again.

Taking a deep breath, she zipped up her bag and headed to the living room where Kyle was waiting, muscles coiled tight.

How could his presence be both reassuring and terrifying?

"Ready?" He asked, gruffly.

She nodded.

They walked outside into the hazy twilight. The peaceful neighborhood seemed at odds with the upheaval inside her and her tiny home.

Kyle opened the passenger door of his sleek black Range Rover. Emma slid in, comforted by the smell of his leather seats and sandalwood cologne. The leather smell was new, but the sandalwood cologne...that hadn't changed. It was the smell of 'home.'

As Kyle slid behind the wheel, Emma felt the faintest flicker of hope. Maybe this was their chance to find closure, forgiveness, and they'd finally be able to move on.

However, as Kyle continued to drive in heavy silence, Emma felt her nerves start to fray. Maybe this wasn't their chance at clearing the air. Maybe this really was just his sense of duty and guilt driving him.

Kyle kept his gaze fixed on the road. The tension hanging between them was stifling.

Emma broke the silence first. "Thank you for staying with me during all of that mess. You didn't have to do that."

Kyle's jaw clenched. "I wasn't going to just leave you alone to deal with it."

"Still. It was kind of you."

Kyle exhaled sharply. "Don't mistake this for kindness. I was just doing the right thing."

Emma flinched at his brusque tone.

That's what she was hoping wasn't the case.

They drove on in strained silence. Emma's gaze drifted to Kyle's muscular forearms and the way his t-shirt clung to his broad chest. She remembered how safe those arms used to make her feel.

Get it together.

Ogling her ex-husband was pointless. No matter how tempting he was, she couldn't let herself be seduced by nostalgia. Too much damage had been done. Even if the past called to her, the future could never be what she wished.

Emma turned to stare out the passenger window, watching the familiar streets of her city roll by. She should feel relieved to be leaving the disturbing scene at her house behind, but an uneasy feeling still churned in the pit of her stomach.

"So, this wasn't the first threatening note?" Kyle asked, taking her by surprise.

Emma sighed. "No. There have been other letters over the past few weeks. Strange phone calls too. Hang ups in the middle of the night."

She saw Kyle's grip on the steering wheel tighten, his knuckles turning white.

"Why didn't you install a security system?" He quizzed.

"Lots of my author friends get stuff like that. They never amount to anything," Emma said, defensively.

Kyle slammed his palm against the steering wheel in frustration. "Damnit, Emma! If you would have taken it seriously, this never would have happened."

Emma looked down at her lap and back out the window, anywhere but at him. "I know. I just…I didn't want to worry anyone. I thought if I just ignored it, they'd eventually stop."

Kyle let out an exasperated sigh. "Yeah, that worked out well."

Emma bristled at his condescending tone. "I can take care of myself, Kyle. Just let me out here. I'll call one of the girls."

"Oh yeah? And bring this trouble into their lives? Fuck, half of them have kids," Kyle shot back.

Emma turned her head to glare at him. As much as she hated to admit it, he had a point. If he hadn't shown up when he did, she didn't know what she would have done. Probably ran crying up onto a neighbor's porch. The police would have been called for sure. On her.

Kyle reached over and put a hand on her shoulder. His touch was electric, sending little sparks dancing across her skin.

"Hey," he said, his voice softening. "It's just...frustrating. And scary."

Emma nodded, not trusting her voice. She was hyper aware of Kyle's hand still resting on her shoulder, his thumb idly stroking her collarbone. She suppressed the shiver at the contact, hating how her body was betraying her, trying to react to his touch despite everything.

This was dangerous territory. She needed to remember that as comforting as Kyle's presence felt right now, at the end of the day, he still hated her.

Some rifts just ran too deep to mend.

Kyle pulled into the driveway of a modest two-story house. It was in a quiet neighborhood on the opposite side of town just over the border into Agawam, surrounded by trees that lent it a secluded, private feel. It didn't hurt that several country clubs were nearby.

He turned off the engine and angled his body towards Emma. "Look, I know things are...complicated between us. But you can't stay in your house until the cops figure this out. It's not safe."

Emma bit her lip, avoiding the intensity of his gaze. As much as she hated to admit it, he had a point. But the thought of staying under the same roof as Kyle made her stomach flutter with nerves. There were so many unresolved feelings between them that it felt like a recipe for disaster.

"I don't know, Kyle. I'll just get a hotel room or something," she mumbled halfheartedly.

Kyle sighed, irritably. "Don't be ridiculous. I have plenty of room here. Save the cash for the lawyer when you sue the fucker that violated your home. Plus, you shouldn't be alone right now."

Kyle might still loathe her, but it was nowhere near the hatred that he felt towards her unknown terrorizer.

"Forced proximity trope, check." Emma mumbled to the window.

"What?" His deep voice was confused, whether because he couldn't hear what she said or didn't understand why she said it, she couldn't tell.

"Nothing."

His voice dropped lower as he added, "Please, Emma. Just get in the house."

The quiet urgency in his tone sent a shiver down her spine. She knew she should refuse, keep her distance like she'd been trying to do. But the memory of the wrecked house and chilling note overpowered her logic. As much as she hated feeling dependent on anyone, the thought of Kyle's solid strength beside her was undeniably reassuring.

"Okay," she conceded softly. "But just until the cops figure this out. I don't want to impose any longer than necessary."

Kyle looked relieved. "You won't hear an argument from me."

His words sent a complicated mix of emotions swirling through her. Gratitude, sadness, longing...dangerous emotions she didn't want to tango with.

"Well...thank you," she said simply. "I appreciate you letting me stay...after everything."

With that, she stepped out of the truck, steeling herself as she followed Kyle inside. She had a feeling these coming days weren't going to be easy.

Kyle unlocked the front door of his sleek modern house and stepped aside to let Emma in first. She hovered in the foyer, taking in the wide-open floor plan and simple, masculine décor. It felt strange, almost intrusive, to be standing in his private space.

Kyle scrutinized her tentative body language. "Make yourself at home. Mi casa es su casa and all that."

Emma nodded, moving slowly into the living room, taking in the stark space. This didn't match with what she remembered of Kyle.

At all.

Kyle watched her for a moment and then headed into the kitchen. "You want something to drink? I've got water, beer..."

"Water is fine, thanks."

He filled two glasses from the fridge dispenser and brought them into the living room. He handed one to her and stepped back, sipping at his own while keeping an eye on her.

An awkward silence descended.

Emma raised her own glass to her lips.

She should say something, anything, but her mind went blank.

Finally, Kyle broke the silence with a safe-ish topic. "So...tell me more about these phone calls you've been getting."

Emma let out a relieved breath and launched into an explanation, grateful to focus on the stalker issue rather than the charged energy humming between them. As she talked, she felt herself relaxing slightly despite the topic at hand. Having Kyle around, solid and dependable as ever, already made her feel safer.

She could do this.

They could get through the next few days if they just focused on the problem at hand.

Everything else – the past, their unresolved feelings – could wait. Maybe forever.

CHAPTER FIVE

September 29, Wednesday
Kyle

The smell of eggs and bacon woke Kyle from a restless sleep. He shuffled into the kitchen, eyes half-open, and paused in the doorway. There was Emma, hair piled in a messy bun, swaying gently at the stove as she hummed along to a pop song playing from her phone.

The domestic scene felt so familiar, yet so foreign at the same time.

"Morning," Emma said, glancing over her shoulder. "I had a car service come and take me home, so I could grab my car. Then I ran to the store and picked up some things to tide me over in the meantime. Oh, also, I made breakfast. Protein-packed omelets with kale and turkey bacon."

He forgot how much of a morning person she was.

Kyle grunted in reply and sank into a chair at the table, not fully comprehending the surreal situation. Emma placed a plate and a glass of orange juice in front of him with a smile.

"Not your usual Pop Tarts and energy drink, huh?" She was giving him a tentative smile that made him grit his teeth.

It made him feel like the bad guy in this situation.

He wasn't! He wasn't the one who broke them apart.

Rather than lashing out, again, something he still felt guilty about...Kyle stared down at the meticulously arranged omelets and neatly lined up strips of turkey bacon. It looked...healthy.

When did Emma start eating like this?

As she plopped down at the table as well, he raised an eyebrow at her waiting glass of water.

No orange juice for her? It was her freaking favorite.

Well…it used to be.

Regardless, as much as he didn't want to, he had to give her some news that was sure to erase the tentative smile from her face.

"I, uh, I don't eat meat anymore. So that's all yours."

She blinked at him and her mouth fell open.

Yeah, meat was a pretty big part of his life back in the day.

"Yeah, I went vegetarian a few years ago. Some of the guys on the team turned me on to it. I perform a lot better now. There's a great documentary on it that we can—"

He cut himself off. They weren't spending any more time together than was necessary.

They weren't friends.

This wasn't *forgiveness.*

This was being a good human and making sure she didn't die. Because as much as he hated her, he loved her once. 'Death' and 'Emma' did not belong in the same sentence.

Ever.

No matter how mad he was at her.

Her soft blue eyes were wide as he scooped up the various meat bits and placed them on the side of his plate. He nodded to them and said, "all yours."

She pursed her lips together…fuck, she did that a lot…and shook her head before turning back to the counter next to the stove.

As Emma sat down across from him with her own plate, Kyle's eyes involuntarily drifted over her body. She was wearing yoga pants that hugged her slim frame and a loose tank top. Had she always been that thin? A small niggle of worry tightened in his gut as he inspected her. No, she was *never* that slight. She was 5'9" and he'd bet his entire salary that she didn't weigh over 120 lbs.

However, as she bit heartily into her own omelets, his gut loosened. So, maybe an eating disorder hadn't plagued her in their time apart? But still, something was different. Something had changed.

Granted, the changes were subtle, but they were still unnerving. He didn't know this version of her.

Kyle ate slowly, occasionally sneaking glances at Emma over his plate. She seemed relaxed. Content even. Meanwhile, his stomach was in knots. How could she act so normal when he could barely look at her without being hit by a wave of hurt and anger? The more he studied her, the more his resentment grew. She had moved on so easily while his life had been completely turned upside down.

As if sensing his shifting mood, Emma's eyes met his. For a moment, Kyle thought he saw a flash of sadness there, but it was quickly replaced with a neutral smile.

"I have a yoga class in twenty minutes, but I'll clean up before I go," she said, standing to clear their plates. She hadn't eaten any of the meat either.

Kyle watched her move gracefully around the kitchen. Yoga class. Of course. Just another one of the *new Emma*'s healthy habits. Meanwhile, his day would consist of a tough workout with the team, strategy meetings, and film review. The contrast between who they were now and who they once were couldn't be starker.

Quietly, Emma finished washing the dishes before giving him a small wave and leaving for her class.

All while Kyle sat alone at the table, lost in thought.

She was here, but at the same time, she wasn't. The woman he loved was gone, replaced by a stranger with a meticulous schedule, perfectly styled hair, kale omelets, and yoga pants.

He almost wished she would yell at him, pick a fight...anything to get a reaction out of the new Zen Emma. But she remained calm, polite. Distant.

With a heavy sigh, Kyle scraped back his chair and headed to the bedroom to change for practice. Just his first day of living with the physical ghost that had haunted him for years.

Kyle grabbed his gym bag and headed out the door, his familiar routine giving him a sense of comfort. At least on the field, things made sense. He knew his role, his purpose.

Unlike how he felt in this sick and twisted dance with Emma.

When Chloe finally got back to him and tentatively told him Emma's address, laced with a series of warnings, he didn't waste any time in doing a drive-by to check it out. Luckily, he knew the neighborhood well because an ex of his had lived there. And judging by how Jaz's car was still in her driveway, she still did. Maybe he'd give her a call some night and have her over when Emma was there, so he could show Emma just how 'moved on' he was.

He winced. Despite the appeal of rubbing his dating repertoire in Emma's face, maybe Jaz wasn't the best candidate. Things had ended awkwardly when Jaz got uncomfortable and clingy toward the end...

As Kyle navigated the familiar route to the training facility, his mind drifted to memories of his early relationship with Emma – the passion, the laughter, the way they'd stay up all night talking. He could still picture the mischievous glint in her eye whenever they'd volley teases back and forth. They were so in sync then, two halves of the same whole. Or so he'd thought.

Clearly he'd been wrong, proven by the indifferent woman who now occupied his house. What had changed? Why had the divorce caught him so off-guard? Shouldn't there have been signs? What did he miss?

Anger simmered in his gut as he replayed their last fight, the hurtful words and demands for divorce thrown like grenades.

He pulled into the parking lot, slamming the door harder than necessary. The other players gave him a wide berth as he stomped into the locker room, jaw clenched. He began to roughly tape his wrists, lost in the spiral of his thoughts. Practice would be his release today, a chance to channel these roiling emotions into raw power on the field. He needed to hit something.

Luckily, his position on the team allowed him to do that.

Kyle's heart pounded with anticipation as he stepped onto the football field, the scent of freshly cut grass filling the air. The sun burned high in the sky, casting a warm, bright shine directly onto the field causing his skin to prickle in the heat.

This was his sanctuary, his battleground, where the world – and Emma – ceased to exist.

He jogged over to the huddle of his teammates, as Head Coach Mitchell's voice rang out, sharp and authoritative, outlining the plan for the day.

The drills began, each movement a symphony of muscle memory and adrenaline. He took his stance, feet shoulder-width apart, knees slightly bent, ready to explode into action. The first snap sent the ball flying toward the quarterback and Kyle's reflexes kicked in. He sprinted forward, the turf yielding in clumps to his cleats.

The collision with the defensive line dummies was fierce and exhilarating, his body a living battering ram. His powerful legs churned as he fought to gain ground, to pave the way for his teammates. The impact was bone-jarring, the clash of bodies echoing in his ears, but he welcomed it. It was a reminder that he was alive, in the moment, pushing his limits.

Being a fullback gave him a multi-faceted position on the team: he could be a protector, but he could also handle the ball.

In the next series of plays, with quick footwork, he pivoted and veered to the side, his eyes locked on Ryan, wearing his quarterback red. Again and again, they ran through the play. Demanding perfection. Here, they were all 'try-hards.'

No one was teased or mocked for caring too much.

They all knew what they had given up to get here. No one became a professional athlete without some sort of sacrifice. It was their jobs to make it all worth it.

Another snap came, and he surged forward again, his arms forming a preservative cocoon around the ball. He bulldozed through the defense, a force of nature on a mission.

As the drills continued, he seamlessly transitioned between blocking and receiving, his instincts guiding him. He knew the dance of the field—the rhythm of the plays, the art of deception, the moments of chaos and order. He executed each move with precision, his body responding to the game's ebb and flow.

Kyle grunted in satisfaction as he drove his shoulder into the tackling dummy, sending it flying across the turf. Around him, his teammates cheered and slapped him on the back.

"Damn, Justice! Save some of that for Sunday," Michael, the main running back on the team, chuckled.

Kyle flexed his hands, adrenaline still pumping through his veins. Hitting the dummy had felt good, but it wasn't enough.

The drills ended and Kyle slowed to a stop, chest heaving, sweat trickling down his temples. He wiped his face with the back of his hand, catching his breath as he joined his teammates for a quick huddle. The offensive coordinator, Butch, was lighting into them, demanding perfection, and harping on their weaknesses.

The guy just needed to shut the fuck up. He was lucky as hell that they had John on staff to assist and offer two decades of experience and guidance, otherwise there wasn't a snowball's chance in hell of them performing as well as they had. Not that anyone in management seemed to recognize Butch's abrasive shortcomings.

If the blowhard kept getting in Kyle's face after every play though...

Management would sure as fuck pay attention, then.

Kyle didn't fucking have the patience for Butch's bullshit today.

As they all moved back inside the facility for showers and recovery, Kyle gulped down some water as his thoughts returned to Emma.

Was she 'home' yet?

Was she puttering around his kitchen making a healthy smoothie?

What would it be like if that was how it had always been? If she hadn't ripped his beating heart out, years ago?

An image of her in yoga pants, strawberry hair piled into a beautifully messy bun, came unbidden to his mind and he shook his head, irritated with himself.

The time for daydreaming. That's not how their life had played out. And there was no going back.

He had to focus on the future. His career, his teammates, himself. None of them had fucked him over. Yet.

· · · • · • · • · ·

When Kyle pulled back into his driveway, he noticed Emma's car was parked there, too. She was 'home'. The thought of her being alone near the scene of her desecration made him squeeze his fists and take some deep breaths before he was able to head inside.

"Hey," he called out gruffly as he entered.

"Hi," came Emma's quiet reply from the kitchen. Kyle dropped his gym bag by the door and walked down the hall. Emma stood at the counter blending up a smoothie, just as he'd pictured. Except her hair was down, cascading over her shoulders. She glanced up and gave him a hesitant smile.

"How was practice?" she asked.

"Fine," Kyle said shortly, grabbing a glass and filling it with water from the fridge. He chugged it fast, acutely aware of Emma's eyes on him.

"Is there a race going on that I missed?"

Kyle wiped his mouth. "Nope. Just thirsty."

An awkward silence descended for long enough that he started to feel a little guilty for snapping at her.

Shit.

Kyle's eyes involuntarily dropped to take in Emma's lithe figure in her leggings and tank top. He quickly looked away.

"I'm gonna grab a shower," he muttered, escaping to his bathroom. As the hot water sluiced over him, he thought over their stilted interaction. He hated how unfamiliar everything felt between them now. He missed the easy banter they used to share.

Memories threatened to suck him into a black hole of what-might-have-beens, so he hummed along to Little Texas' other hits instead.

With a sigh, he finished up and wandered into his bedroom. After changing, he went back to the kitchen. Emma was sitting on one of the couches, reading.

"Whatcha got there?" Kyle asked, startling her.

"Oh, hi. Just some research for my next book," Emma said, she had the same vacant expression on her face as she used to when she was lost in a fictional world.

"Cool." Kyle rifled through the takeout menus. "Pizza sound good for dinner?"

Emma licked her lips and looked uncomfortable. "Do they have a spinach salad?"

Kyle blinked in surprise.

No pizza?

That had been one of Emma's main food groups.

"Salad?" He asked. "Are you kidding?"

Emma glanced around, pink blooming on her cheeks, and she shrugged. "I just had a smoothie, and I'm not that hungry – so a salad would be great."

What the fuck?

"Em, you once ranted to an entire restaurant staff that salads were for rabbits. And now you eat them for *dinner*?" He gestured at her. "You've lost a shit ton of weight. You can eat more than a salad."

She stiffened and her nostrils flared. Emma looked like she was going to say something in return but choked it back down. "Just so you know, spinach is rich in antioxidants and ridiculously healthy. But if you're not going to let me go that route without giving me shit, then fine. I'm in the mood for three-bean chili. The more tomatoes, chili powder, and cumin the better. There? Happy?"

There.

There it was.

Her fire. Her spunk.

It was still there – thank God – hiding under that unflappable, put-together mirage.

The relief was blinding.

Kyle dug through the menus before going into the kitchen and calling the orders in. He then refilled their waters and made his way to the opposite couch, flipping on the TV as he sunk down in the cushions.

"Just like old times," he murmured as he reclined back.

That wasn't quite true; they were never more than a foot apart. The whole living room between them now never would have flown back in the day.

But...it wasn't back then...it was now.

She continued to read her book. He continued to try to watch TV. But he was continuously distracted by her tucking falling strands of her hair behind her ear.

Just get a fucking hair tie, Emma!

Or cut it off!

Put it back to what it used to be!

After the take-out arrived, Kyle brought the food to their opposite places and they ate on their couches, the TV providing background noise. For the first time in ages, the silence between them felt comfortable.

As Kyle polished off his last bite, he noticed the rain that had started lashing against the windows.

A rumble of thunder vibrated the panes and the TV's audio spaced out for a second.

Lightning flashed, illuminating Emma's face. She looked thoughtful, her eyes far off.

What was she thinking about?

Kyle studied Emma's profile in the flickering TV light.

A myriad of feelings warred within him, but one stood out – no matter how much had changed between them, some connections couldn't be broken. Not completely.

Their relationship hung suspended – which way the wind would blow it next, remained to be seen.

Would he ever find out what caused her to destroy their lives?

Or was he better off not knowing?

Chapter Six

September 30, Friday
Emma

The next day, Emma tightened her grip on the steering wheel as she pulled into the parking lot of the doctor's office. Her palms were clammy, and her heart pounded in her chest. She took a deep breath, trying to calm her racing thoughts. It was just a checkup – nothing more, nothing less.

Get it together.

She rubbed at her face before she stepped out of her car and locked the doors. The chilly autumn breeze brushed against her face, bringing a small shiver down her spine. She walked towards the arched entrance, her shoes clicking against the pavement. Each step felt too loud.

Emma stepped into the bland, beige waiting room, an antiseptic smell immediately assaulting her nostrils. She suppressed a shudder, memories of long hospital stays flashing through her mind. It didn't matter how many times she came for checkups; she was always met with the same sense of drowning.

The walls were painted a stark white, devoid of any cheerful artwork. The fluorescent lighting cast an eerie glow over the room, accentuating the tension that hung heavy in the air.

When walking in, she saw an elderly man to her left who seemed lost in thought and on her right, a young couple held hands tightly, their knuckles white from tension.

Her mind wandered to Kyle. If he knew what she was going through, would he be here, holding her hand like that young couple? Or would his stubborn pride keep them apart?

The receptionist behind the counter looked up from her computer screen, offering a tight smile. "Good morning, Emma. Dr. Thompson will be with you shortly."

Yeah, she was on a first name basis with the receptionist. It was fun.

"Thanks," Emma replied, her voice barely above a whisper. She glanced around the room, before moving toward the corner, trying not to make eye contact with anyone else in the waiting room. Seeing their hollow-eyed looks and wrapped heads always brought back a wave of terror and trauma. Better if she kept her eyes on the floor.

As Emma took a seat, she closed her eyes for a moment, trying to block out the harsh reality of her surroundings.

Happy thoughts, happy thoughts, happy thoughts.

She thought of Kyle and their newfound...truce.

Maybe truce was too strong of a word.

But it had been several days at this point, with no news from the police, and Kyle didn't say anything last night when she mentioned moving back home. He gave her a tired look, shook his head, and gave her a short grunt. "No" was all he said.

And that was apparently that.

She wasn't all that hyped up to live with him either, but the masochist...or maybe sadist...in her couldn't make herself leave.

Not yet.

Not before seeing if she could find a way to lessen a little bit of the hurt she saw haunting his dark eyes.

"Emma Potter?" A feminine voice called out, breaking her reverie.

She opened her eyes and looked up, meeting the gaze of Dr. Thompson. No nurse today. She was brought directly to the big kahuna.

Ready or not.

Taking another deep breath, Emma rose from her chair and followed the doctor into the examination room, her heart pounding with every step.

Dr. Thompson pulled back a curtain and gestured for her to take a seat on the paper-covered examination table. "All right, Emma. You know the drill."

That she did.

"Sure thing, Doc," Emma moved behind the curtain and stripped quickly. Modesty didn't exist for her and her doctors anymore.

She wasn't even sure why the other woman even pulled the curtain.

At this point, it was probably just muscle memory.

"Just promise me we can skip the part where you tell me I have two weeks to live." Emma gave a weak laugh that sounded false even to her own ears.

"Very funny," the doctor responded, her eyes crinkling sadly at the corners. "But don't worry, I save those for my Monday appointments."

Taking a deep breath, Emma steadied her nerves before speaking. "I know it might sound a bit...excessive because I had a checkup a few months ago, but...I want to request another body scan."

She hadn't made this appointment for the fun of it. Symptoms were rearing their ugly head again. And although the itchiness in her breast could be nothing more than a yeast infection, and the lump could be harmless swelling caused by hormones...Something wasn't right.

She tried to tell herself she was overreacting, but deep down she *knew*.

"At your last check, your cell counts were *slightly* lower than we'd like to see. And your inflammatory markers were *slightly* elevated, indicating your immune system was working overtime against something. We discussed that at the time and thought maybe it was related to you catching something. But maybe not." The doctor paused, meeting Emma's gaze. "I don't want you to panic. This doesn't mean anything definitive yet. But we'll take some blood work again today to see if there has been any change. Let's see what I can find after a little poking around, too, shall we?"

Dr. Thompson approached Emma, who was now lying horizontal on the table. The doctor started with a series of quick, non-invasive touches to Emma's neck, navel and armpits.

Then came the fun part.

Dr. Thompson pulled her hospital johnny down and exposed her left breast. Or...what was left of it.

"Last time, I was caught off guard by my diagnosis," Emma explained. "I just want to be sure that we're not missing anything this time around. Things have been *off* lately."

The other woman nodded, moved to the other breast, and started her finger massages there.

Emma felt the doctor's fingers still as she encountered where she thought she felt a lump.

So, it wasn't just her imagination. It was small, but it was there.

Emma squeezed her eyes tight and breathed hard, trying not to sob.

A few more minutes of silent poking and the johnny was raised back up.

"All right," the doctor said, nodding again and moving to the sink to rewash her hands. "I see what you mean. Has anything changed since we talked on the phone last week? Any change in symptoms?"

Emma sat up and shook her head, unable to form words, her breath caught in her throat.

Dr. Thompson rattled off more questions while making notes on the computer. Finally, she said, "I'll put in an order for a PET scan. I know one of the machines is down and the other has a bit of a waitlist, but I'll see what I can do. And again, I'd also like to run some blood work, too."

This was it. This was it all over again.

Emma's hands started shaking and she gripped them together tightly.

She swallowed hard. The cancer was back and this time, she might not be so lucky.

"I know the waiting is difficult," the doctor said gently. "But we'll get to the bottom of this. Don't lose hope."

Hope was such a fickle thing when you had stared death in the face before.

She stifled the insane laugh that bubbled up and channeled her inner Kyle.

Tackle today.

"I'll send an order to the labs. Head on down and they'll get you right in. I'll also have a nurse call you with some tentative scan dates." She leaned in as if imparting a secret. "Staffing has been impossible and the temp we have up front for scheduling will probably slot you for next year. You'll have better luck with one of the nurses."

Emma nodded and tried to not look like she was falling apart.

Apparently she succeeded because she and Dr. Thompson said her goodbyes and left the room.

One foot in front of the other – and it truly was all she could do to put one foot in front of the other on her way to the lab.

On autopilot, Emma took a seat and tried to block out the panic in her head.

She kept replaying the doctor's words in her head. Lower blood cell counts. Elevated inflammatory markers. Investigate further.

Man, she hated this place. They always missed her veins and blamed it on them 'rolling.'

When she had lived in New Hampshire, the oncology team she had for her original battle with cancer was top notch. She loved the hospital in Lebanon. Their phlebotomists never missed...

"Emma?"

She glanced up. The nurse held a tray of vials and tubes.

Emma swallowed thickly and stood. She followed the nurse down another sterile hallway to the phlebotomy room. The tourniquet cinched tight around her arm, cutting off circulation. The smell of alcohol swabs stung her nose as the nurse readied the needle.

Emma turned her head, biting her lip at the sharp prick in her arm.

"Oops. Darn it. Sucker moved on me. Hold tight, let's try again."

Poke.

"Son of a— "

Another poke.

"There we go."

Dark red blood flowed into the glass vials. She thought of all the times she'd endured this, willing her body to heal. How alone she felt. How angry she was.

It was all coming back.

She still had so much life left to live!

Emma longed to call Kyle, to find comfort in his strong arms. But she couldn't burden him now, at the height of his career. This was her battle to face. Again. Just like before.

She'd said it a thousand times. The universe had a sick sense of humor. Bringing them back together, even in their tense capacity, just to rip them apart again.

The nurse finished filling the vials and removed the needle, pressing a cotton ball to Emma's arm.

"All done. The doctor or nurse will reach out if necessary."

Emma simply nodded, unable to find her voice.

She made her way back to the front entrance and left the imposing brick building. The bright afternoon sun seemed to mock her situation as she squinted against the glare. Emma clutched her purse tightly, the leather digging into her palm as she tried to process the uncertainty that now clouded her future.

Maybe she was overreacting.

Maybe she was totally fine.

Her fingers combed through her strawberry blonde locks in a futile attempt to find comfort. She didn't want to lose everything that she'd gained.

But if the cancer was back, she would beat it. She had to.

"Hey, Emma!" A familiar voice called out from behind her in the lobby, snapping her out of her spiraling thoughts. "You all right? You look like you've seen a ghost."

Oh, Jeeze. Emma turned and saw Jen approaching with her signature sporty walk.

Crap.

She was not in the right headspace to carry on a conversation.

"Hey," Emma forced a trembling smile to her lips. "I'm good. I just don't like hospitals." She looked into Jen's concerned amber eyes, wishing she could tell her everything. But she didn't want to burden her with her drama.

"Same, they suck." Jen paused and looked at her closer. "Are you sure? You look wrecked..." Jen asked, her piercing gaze unwavering as it searched Emma's face.

"Nah, I just have a real phobia of needles and had to get some routine blood work done. Just recovering from that."

What was a small white lie between friends?

Emma held up her elbow to show the band aid in the crook of her elbow as supporting evidence.

Jen nodded, her face turning understanding. "I get that. There's one guy here that always misses the vein..." Jen trailed off and then her energy picked right back up again. "Oh! By the way, have the police found any leads yet? I haven't seen Kyle yet this morning to ask him."

Ugh! She could have just blamed her expression on the break in! She didn't need to get into her hospital phobia. She felt like face palming.

"Oh, yeah, no. No news yet. They want me to come in next week and look at some mugshots but I'm not too optimistic. I'd like to go back home but Kyle's demanding I call his buddy that installs security systems, first." Emma replied, swallowing hard and praying her voice wouldn't betray her. "Otherwise, nothing too thrilling going on in my life."

Jen's eyes still held a flicker of concern. "That's not thrilling and overwhelming to you? Kudos. I'd be a wreck. When my apartment was trashed, I damn near went catatonic. I fought John hard to let me find a separate place to live." She paused and whispered, "the cat part was fucked up. Kyle told me about it when I was working on his ankle yesterday." She looked around before bringing her eyes back to Emma. Jen lowered her voice as if to impress upon Emma the sincerity of her statement. "If you're ever feeling overwhelmed or need someone to talk to, don't hesitate to call me, okay? I can keep a secret. I can listen. I can be a sounding board. I can be whatever. But don't be an island, okay? I worry about you."

"Thank you," Emma whispered, trying hard not to cry. Her emotions were already on a precipice, they didn't need Jen being awesome to topple them over.

They said their goodbyes and Emma made her way out to the small parking garage where her car was parked off 91 and slid behind the wheel. She rested her forehead against the steering wheel and tried to slow her racing heart.

Despite the doctor's reassurances, she couldn't shake the sinking feeling in her gut.

Flashes of memory assaulted her – endless days spent curled up in pain, violent nausea after rounds of chemo, the fear that each breath might be her last.

She had been so young then, so determined to fight. She wasn't sure she had that same fire now. And she couldn't tell Kyle, not when he was living his dream. That would be as unfair now as it would have been then.

A sob ripped out of her, and she wrapped her arms around her chest and held herself tight. She rocked slowly side to side as the cries rippled through her body. Emma let it consume her, let the loud cries and gasps echo about in her small car.

What if the cancer was more aggressive this time? What if it had already spread too far?

She thought of the life she had built – her writing career finally taking off, plans to start a family someday, Sunday mornings spent horseback riding to clear her mind. It was everything she had dreamed of.

Now it all might slip through her fingers.

After several minutes, the tears subsided. With a shuddering breath, Emma swiped the tears from her cheeks. She had made it through this once before. If the worst happened, she would find the strength to fight again. She had to believe that.

She thought of calling Jen, taking her up on her offer, but couldn't bring herself to say the words out loud. To speak of it made it real and she was still processing. Maybe tomorrow.

With trembling hands, Emma wiped at her eyes one more time, started the car, and pulled out of the parking lot. As she drove, she repeated the same thought over and over.

In a few weeks she would know for sure. A few weeks of carrying this agonizing weight in her heart. Then she'd have her answers.

Tackle today.

CHAPTER SEVEN

October 2, Sunday
Emma

Two days later, the sun dipped below the horizon, casting an orange glow through the living room windows. Emma stood in the kitchen, chopping vegetables for dinner, trying to ignore the heavy silence that had settled like a thick fog between Kyle and her. Occasionally, she'd sneak a glance at him, hunched over his laptop on the couch, his brow furrowed as he focused on whatever task he was working on.

"Any news from the police?" Emma ventured, desperate for any scrap of conversation to fill the void.

"Nothing yet," Kyle muttered without looking up. His eyes remained fixed on the screen, but Emma could sense his tension, even from across the room.

Despite the uncomfortable atmosphere, they were making an effort to maintain some semblance of normalcy in their strange cohabitation. They ate together, watched TV in the evenings, and occasionally exchanged small talk about their days. But it was a delicate balancing act – one wrong word or lingering glance could send them toppling back into the abyss of unresolved feelings and heartache.

Over the last few days, Emma noticed that the house seemed to grow more comfortable. It wasn't as if the walls themselves had changed, but rather the way they moved within those walls. The air felt lighter, less suffocating, as if they had both exhaled a breath they'd been holding for far too long.

Which, given how the weekend had started for her, was a miracle.

Kyle joined Emma in the kitchen one evening, grabbing a beer from the fridge before leaning against the counter, watching her cook. There was still a guardedness to his posture, but he seemed more at ease than he had been before.

"Need help with anything?" He asked, taking a swig of his drink.

"Sure," Emma replied, handing him a cutting board and knife. "You can chop the onions."

As they worked side by side, the familiar rhythm of their past life together began to reassert itself. They moved around each other with ease, the tension slowly fading, replaced by something else entirely – a fragile, unspoken truce.

"Thanks for helping with dinner," Emma murmured as they sat down to eat. She avoided his gaze, focusing on her plate instead.

"Sure," Kyle replied, his voice soft and unexpectedly gentle.

In those quiet moments, sharing their living space more comfortably than ever before, Emma couldn't help but wonder if there was still hope for them – a chance to heal their wounds and move forward together, despite everything that had happened.

Not romantically, her upcoming scan would show that would only end tragically.

But as friends. Exes. Maybe just people who *used to be* friends.

Maybe, at the very least, the hatred could be healed.

If she was going to die...she'd like to know she wouldn't go with him hating her.

Emma sat on the couch, her legs curled beneath her as she flipped through a trashy magazine. She twirled her hair and she nibbled absently at her lower lip as she scanned the gossip stories.

"Still reading those things?" Kyle asked, joining her in the living room. He stretched his legs out, resting his socked feet on the coffee table with a groan.

Woah, he was almost touching her. Big moment.

"Old habits die hard," Emma replied with a teasing smile. "Plus, I find really fun inspiration in here. Storylines, characters, outfits. That kind of thing."

"Ah, obviously it's all for research."

"Hey, it's not all fluff," she retorted, playfully swatting him with the glossy pages. "There are some genuinely interesting articles in here."

"Like that piece on the top five ways to rock a messy bun?" Kyle raised an eyebrow, chuckling at her mock indignation.

"Exactly," she shot back, lips twitching. "Life-changing stuff, really. How else would I know how to look effortlessly chic while doing household chores?"

Their chuckles filled the room, a sound so familiar it sent a shiver down Emma's spine. As their laughter subsided, they shared a brief, soft look, before quickly averting their gazes.

Emma felt her cheeks flush and her breath hitch in her throat.

"Remember when we used to have movie nights?" Kyle asked softly, almost hesitantly. "When we'd stay up way too late watching terrible rom coms, eating popcorn and drinking cheap wine?"

"God, that wine was awful," Emma grimaced, but her eyes sparkled with nostalgia. "But yes, I remember. Those are some of my favorite memories."

"Mine too," he admitted, his dark eyes searching hers. There was a vulnerability in his gaze that she hadn't seen before, and it both terrified and thrilled her.

"Maybe we could," she hesitated, her heart pounding, "do that again sometime? You know, for...research...on story structure."

"Sure," the word was dragged out of him. "We could maybe try that."

"Prepare yourself for some truly awful cinema, then," she warned, trying out a grin despite the turmoil of emotions swirling inside her.

As they sat there, inches apart yet worlds away, Emma couldn't help but feel the pull between them – the magnetic tension that had always existed, even when they tried to ignore it. She knew she should resist, but as the sun set and the room grew darker, the shadows seemed to whisper promises of what might have been, and what could still be if they dared to take a chance.

No. The lump in her breast and the likelihood of recurrence meant she couldn't. No matter how badly she might want to. She *couldn't* keep hurting him.

Even if it was just fatty tissue this time...what about next time...or the time after that?

With a small, sad smile, Emma looked back down at her magazine and tried to ignore the heat of Kyle's probing gaze.

CHAPTER EIGHT

October 5, Wednesday
Emma

Days later, Emma stood in the kitchen, sunlight streaming through the open window. The TV played a sports channel in the background, filling the silence with a cutting analysis of the latest plays and the men that made them. She couldn't help but smile as she watched Kyle working his way through a stack of dirty dishes.

"Never thought I'd see the day when Kyle Justice willingly washes dishes," she teased, leaning against the counter.

"Hey, I've matured," he shot back, grinning as he scrubbed a plate. "I also put my clothes in the hamper now. Did you know that the lid on top actually opens?"

"Goodness no! Really?" Emma feigned innocence, raising an eyebrow.

"Took thirty-two years but I finally learned it." He paused. "I know how much that used to bug you."

"You think? How many times did we fight about it?" She chuckled, surprised by his unexpected friendliness. "Anyway, I'm glad you found one of the secrets to life. It's transformative."

"Progress is what we're all about here," Kyle replied, a hint of sarcasm in his tone. But as their laughter faded, Emma found herself studying him – this new version of the man she once knew so well.

The way his dark hair fell across his forehead, the strength and confidence in his movements, the kindness that lingered in his eyes when he thought no one was watching. Beneath the bitter exterior, there were glimpses of the real Kyle, and it fascinated her. Yet, she was still so torn. She wanted to share her story with him and explain why she had hurt him so deeply, but she knew it would only cause more pain.

So, silence it was.

Even though it made her heart ache.

As they continued working together around the house – cleaning, laundry, dishes,

cooking – Emma found herself both amazed and intimidated by the changes in Kyle. He was still fiercely protective and loyal, but there was a newfound patience and understanding there.

Once he stopped remembering that he hated her for breaking his heart, that is.

"Hey," Kyle said, interrupting her thoughts as they stood in the dining room in front of the patio doors, surveying their handiwork. "That went a lot quicker with four hands."

"Imagine that," she chuckled.

He turned his head to the backyard and looked out at the trees that lined his property. "It is pretty great, isn't it?"

"Definitely," Emma agreed.

What would their life have been like if she had been more honest?

He certainly wouldn't be playing for the Spartans.

"Kyle?" she whispered, her voice barely audible over the sound of rustling leaves coming through the open windows.

"Yeah?"

"Thank you...for trying. For giving us a chance to be civil with each other, despite everything."

"I was an asshole when I saw you again, this is my way of making up for that." He wasn't wrong, but she did also blindside him, so she was willing to take that hit. He always did have a hot temper when he felt cornered. "Plus, a hotel wouldn't have been safe – staying with me was the only sound option."

She cocked her head as she looked at him. It *wasn't* the only option – a hotel would have been fine. He was just worried. Despite her tearing out his heart and his asshole behavior at the diner, he was still

Kyle. Her Kyle. And her Kyle never would have let her stay in a hotel where he couldn't work to keep her safe. Even after a nasty breakup – not when her life was on the line.

"Still," she murmured, tucking a lock of hair behind her ear. "Thanks."

He cleared his throat and gestured toward the patio. "Take a seat? I'll grab us some wine. The good kind. I don't stock the cheap shit anymore."

Relieved and floating in a bubble of peace, Emma nodded and made her way outside and onto a cozy looking chair. One that was entirely too small for Kyle.

The past few days had been filled with moments of surprising connection, and although they were still guarded around each other, there was a sense that something was shifting between them.

"Did the girls tell you that I almost got arrested for public indecency a few years ago?" Kyle asked, sipping his wine and keeping his eyes trained on the far away trees.

"Definitely not," she laughed, shaking her head. "Do I even want to know?"

"Probably not, but I'll tell you anyway." He leaned back in his chair, eyes twinkling with mischief. "So, after the Spartans threw stupid money at me, I went through a bit of a wild phase. One night, I decided it would be a great idea to streak across the stadium. Really introduce myself to my new home, you know."

"Kyle!" Emma gasped, giggling in secondhand embarrassment. "You didn't! You were twenty-eight! You couldn't have been that stupid."

"Yup, I was. Got caught by security halfway across the field, buck naked and reeking of beer. Luckily, Coach Butch was there and talked them out of sending me to the drunk tank. Instead, he drove me home and chewed me out, himself."

"Wow," she said, trying to suppress a smile. "You're an idiot." That about summed it up.

"Yeah, I never claimed to be an angel," he replied, raising an eyebrow. "Although, these days, I do try to keep my clothes on in public."

"Unless it's a charity photo shoot for a very exclusive calendar..." Emma mumbled playfully, taking another sip of her wine with a coy smile on her face.

"You heard about that?"

Was that a blush blooming on his tawny skin?

Well, that was adorable.

She looked at him, really looked at him, and felt a pang of regret for all the years they'd lost.

"Yeah, I'll strip down nowadays for a good charity. I actually did one a few months ago for an ex." He paused and looked over at her. "Jaz was wicked into books too." His lips twisted in a sardonic grin. "I'm starting to wonder if I have a type."

Ugh, why did mentioning his ex make her want to commit homicide? Clearly, the man wasn't a cloistered nun in their time apart, but jeeze...he didn't have to *talk* about it.

Then again, even though he was mentioning his ex, causing her to want to choke this poor unknown woman...his lowered gaze and comment felt almost like...flirting.

Chills ran down her skin and butterflies danced in her belly.

"Anyway," Kyle continued, his voice softening, "I've been working on something lately that might interest you. You remember how you always used to talk about starting a children's literacy program back home?"

"Of course," Emma breathed, her eyes widening. "Why? What have you been doing?"

"Every year since I got drafted, I've been sending money back to our old school district," he admitted, his cheeks flushing even more. "I started a scholarship fund for underprivileged kids who want to study literature or writing."

"Kyle, that's…amazing," she whispered, her heart swelling with pride and affection.

And then he went and ruined the moment.

"Even though we were the big failure that everyone said we'd be, we're still not doing too bad for ourselves. So that's something." He shrugged, attempting nonchalance. "Hell, I've traveled the world. Made millions. Donated a shit ton. Dated everyone from bookworms, to supermodels, to lawyers, to actresses. And you achieved your dream of being a best-selling author. So, maybe the town just saw what we couldn't – that we still had a lot of life left to live and it just couldn't be lived together."

His words landed like knife stabs. Ripping her apart slowly.

They had something special.

Life changing.

And here he was, referencing it like it had been nothing.

Emma wanted to scream at him, tell him he was wrong. That they were soulmates, but that cancer had other plans. She wanted to roar the truth at him, tell him that she broke up with him to save him. To save him the pain, suffering, and distraction that her treatment would cause. Successful treatment or not, she didn't want to ruin his future.

She tried to hold back the tears that were threatening to spill over and ruin her carefully put-together façade. She knew she couldn't show him how much his words were affecting her.

"Sounds like you've been living quite the life," she said quietly, looking away from him and focusing on the sunset. As the sky turned a brilliant shade of orange, she couldn't help but think of all the sunsets they'd missed together, all the moments lost to time and heartbreak. "You're doing it all." Her voice was steady, but inside she was crumbling.

And as the sun finally slipped beneath the horizon, she wished – not for the first time – that she had never gotten cancer.

The silence stretched between them like a taut string, fragile and ready to snap. Emma could feel her heart splintering with each passing second, knowing just how much pain she'd caused him. But there he was, living his dreams and thriving despite it all. It should have made her happy, but instead, it only served to strengthen her resolve in keeping the truth from him.

"Looks like you've been happy," Emma murmured, unable to keep the wistful longing out of her voice. "Achieving your dream."

Kyle paused, staring at her with an intensity that made her breath catch. His eyes were dark and fierce, filled with equal parts pain and determination.

"*You* were my dream," he replied, his voice barely above a whisper.

Emma's heart clenched painfully at his words, tears threatening to spill over as she struggled to find a response. But what could she say? How could she make him understand that everything she'd done had been to protect him, even if it meant breaking them both in the process?

They sat there, suspended in time, as the world around them faded into insignificance. All that remained was the raw, unspoken truth that hung heavy in the air between them.

As the seconds ticked by, Emma finally found her voice, forcing herself to speak through the pain. "I'm sorry, Kyle," she said quietly, her eyes never leaving his. "I never wanted to hurt you."

The silence that followed felt like an eternity, as if the universe itself held its breath in anticipation of what would come next. But in the end, all they had were the unspoken words and the lingering ache of dreams left unfulfilled. And so, they sat across from each other, a vast expanse between them, bound together by a love that refused to fade, even as the world moved on around them.

CHAPTER NINE

October 5, Wednesday Night
Emma

Long after the sun had disappeared, Emma wandered inside and washed out her wine glass in the sink. He had come inside behind her but still hadn't said a word as he waited for her to move. Emma's heart ached more fiercely, the weight of her unsaid words threatening to crush her.

As Emma moved out of his way, their eyes met for fleeting moments before darting away again, as if too afraid to confront the raw emotion simmering beneath the surface. It was a dance of avoidance, an unspoken acknowledgment of the chasm that had opened up between them.

"Pass me the sponge, please," Kyle muttered, breaking the silence that had settled over them like a shroud.

"Sure," Emma replied softly, handing it over and watching him carefully clean the fragile globe of his wine glass.

How he could be so large and strong and still so gentle at the same time...

His muscles flexed beneath his shirt, a testament to the work he did in the gym and in the kitchen. It wasn't just lifting weights but fueling his body too, and he clearly did it well.

Once Kyle placed his glass on the drying mat, they retreated to the living room, their usual banter conspicuously absent. Instead, they fell into their well-worn routine, settling in at opposite ends of the couch to watch a movie as they had done since that Sunday when they discussed it.

The distance between them felt like miles rather than inches, and Emma could feel the heaviness in the air, thick with unspoken words of repressed emotions.

As the opening credits began, she glanced at Kyle, taking in the tense set of his jaw and the way his eyes remained fixed on the screen, refusing to meet hers. Her chest tightened, and she fought back the tears that threatened to escape, unwilling to break the delicate peace they'd managed to establish.

"I'm so sorry, Kyle," she whispered into the darkness, her voice barely audible over the sound of the movie. She could feel the hurt circling her heart, a relentless reminder of the pain she'd caused and the love that still burned between them. "I never meant to hurt you. Not then, and not now."

For a moment, there was nothing but the flickering light from the screen casting shadows on his face, but then he turned to look at her, his eyes searching hers in the dim room. She saw the weight of his own emotions there, a mirror of her own heartache, and for an instant, they were connected in their shared pain.

But as quickly as it had come, the moment passed, leaving them once again adrift in the vast ocean of their unresolved histories.

The movie played on, a distant backdrop to the storm of emotions raging within Emma's heart, as she struggled to come to terms with the truth: that the love they'd once shared would forever be bound by the secrets and lies that had torn them apart.

It was as if the room had grown smaller, the distance between them more pronounced than ever before. But when she felt the burn of Kyle's gaze on her, she turned to look at him and even in the low light it was evident that his eyes shining with unshed tears. "Why?"

The honesty in his question nearly broke her. Her fingers clenched into fists in her lap, and she wished she could just tell him the truth – about the cancer, about how she'd wanted to spare him the pain of living through her illness. But she knew that revealing her secret would only cause more damage, so instead, she simply said, "I was afraid."

"Of what?"

"Of losing everything," she admitted, her heart pounding in her chest. "Of losing you, our future...and myself."

A mix of emotions played across Kyle's face as he digested her words. The air between them seemed to crackle with unspoken tension, and yet neither dared to bridge the gap that separated them.

"Well, Emma," he whispered, "You lost me."

An invisible vacuum sucked the air from her lungs and she struggled to breathe.

This was what death felt like. She was sure of it.

Her vision was blurred by her tears, her throat felt like she had swallowed glass.

Yeah, she had most certainly lost him. And maybe even herself...

"I'm scared, too."

She jolted and looked at him, barely able to discern him through the darkness and the blur of her tears. "Scared of what?"

"Of letting you back in, only for you to break me again."

The vulnerability in his admission took her breath away, and she felt a surge of hope that maybe if nothing else, he could forgive her.

"Kyle," she murmured, her hand reaching out to tentatively cover his, "I—."

What was she supposed to say?

What could she say?

He stared down at her hand on his, and then up in her eyes, as if searching for answers. Then, with a slow nod, he whispered, "All right."

It felt like *forgiveness*.

Like a dam releasing.

Coolness washed through her body and caused her fingers to prick and tingle.

Back when they were together, he'd teased her for being so verbose with her words on paper but so fumbling when it came to speaking them aloud; it seemed like time hadn't changed that. He knew she regretted breaking his heart. The small bob of his head said he didn't need her to voice the words.

Maybe it wasn't true forgiveness, but looking at Kyle's peaceful expression as he stared at the TV, the acceptance there...the acknowledgment...

It was freeing.

CHAPTER TEN

October 6, Thursday
Emma

Emma stared down at the steaming mug of organic ginger tea in her hands, the warm and invigorating aroma doing little to perk up her bleary mood.

Despite her heart to heart with Kyle last night, her mind just wouldn't shut off. Instead of worrying about Kyle forgiving her, now she was worried about what would happen once she found out officially that her cancer was back.

He had offered an olive branch and now she had to decide whether to tear it to shreds by telling him she had cancer, or just walking away from his life again – hopefully this time with no broken hearts.

Except her own.

It was always so easy being with him. She never fell out of love with him, so thinking back on their night warmed her heart and fractured it at the same time. From the effortless way they shared chores, to chatting while sitting on the patio...despite it being on the chair his ex had apparently bought...to their gentle moment on the couch. It all played over again in her mind. All night long.

Across the kitchen island, Kyle grunted, his muscular frame bent over the sports section.

She watched him past the rim of her mug, taking in the curve of his shoulders beneath his t-shirt, the way his hair curled just so against his neck. An old familiarity stirred within her...

And here she was, thinking chemo and radiation had killed her libido.

Kyle turned, catching her staring. Emma looked away quickly, heat flooding her cheeks.

"Hey, would you be cool if I grilled us some veggie burgers for dinner?" he said after a moment.

"Oh, yeah. Sure." Emma smiled tentatively. "I can grab some fixings from the store."

A peace offering, of sorts. Not exactly friends, but no longer enemies under one roof. She could work with that.

Baby steps, she told herself. Baby steps.

Kyle leaned against the counter, sipping his coffee. "So, any big plans for the day?"

Emma shrugged, tracing her finger along the handle of her mug. "I might go swing by the stables. I haven't been out in a few days."

Kyle raised an eyebrow. "I heard you were a big equestrian now."

"I mean, I'm no Julie. I just volunteer there sometimes so I've picked up some small tricks with the horses," she explained. "It's therapeutic. Plus, doing the buddy rides is always a ton of fun. That's where I met Jen, John, and Ryan actually. On one of the therapy outing days." She smiled at the memory. "I don't think they know this still to this day, but Ryan kept pretending he had no idea how to ride a horse to lighten up the tension. The kid can *ride*." Emma looked at Kyle and shrugged. "Working with the kids is a blast and it makes me appreciate my own life a little more, whenever I leave there. The spunk and fight that some of these young kids have...it's inspiring."

Kyle's expression softened. "That's really cool, Em. You always did have a big heart."

Emma's breath caught at the unexpected sincerity in his voice. For a moment, she saw a flash of the old Kyle, the one who knew her better than anyone.

Their eyes met and held. The kitchen suddenly felt suffocating. Emma's heart pounded against her ribs. Slowly, Kyle set down his mug and took a step towards her. His hand lifted, as if to touch her face...

A random car horn blared outside, shattering the moment. They jumped apart. Emma turned quickly, grabbing her purse off the counter.

"I-I better get going," she stammered. "See you tonight."

She hurried out without looking back, pulse racing.

Too close.

She couldn't let herself get swept up again. It was too risky.

They'd just be right back where they started.

No romance, no feelings. Just roommates until it was safe to move home. Then, they would go their separate ways and maybe only ever see each other again in passing at their friends' parties.

Which would be a relief after having five years of strategic avoidant experiences. How she had managed to successfully evade him for so long still amazed her.

Emma took a deep breath as she pulled out of the driveway, trying to calm her racing thoughts.

What if...

What if she told him the truth? What if she came clean about then *and* now?

Emma gripped the steering wheel tight.

No, that would be the epitome of cruelty.

She had to stay strong, keep her distance. This living situation was temporary. Soon the stalker would be caught, and she could move on with her life, without Kyle.

It was better this way.

Cleaner.

Kyle deserved more than she could give him. He deserved to be free of her and the wreckage she'd bring.

Emma arrived at the ranch and busied herself with grooming the horses, trying to ignore the hollow ache in her chest.

As she led a mare named Buttercup into the paddock, Emma steeled her resolve. She would be pleasant but distant with Kyle, keep things light and impersonal between them. No more vulnerable moments.

It was the only way to protect them both.

• • • • • • • • • •

Emma returned to the house later that afternoon, feeling emotionally drained but determined to keep up a friendly façade with Kyle. As she entered the kitchen, the smell of fresh baked cookies wafted through the air.

Kyle stood at the counter, wearing an apron and placing cookies onto a cooling rack. He looked up when Emma walked in, a small smile on his face.

"Hey, I got bored this afternoon and decided to do some baking. It's something I picked up over the years, helps me relax. Want one? I promise I won't poison you. Though it does have protein powder mixed in," he lamely joked.

Kyle's smile faltered for a moment when she hesitated.

Ah, what the hell. The cancer was probably back, anyway. Might as well enjoy a cookie.

"I'd love one, thanks."

Kyle nodded, handing her a cookie. As their fingers brushed, a spark of electricity jolted through Emma's body. She quickly stepped back, heart pounding.

An awkward silence descended as Emma chewed on her warm and gooey treat.

Delicious.

But not as delicious as Kyle in an apron. Woof.

"Anyway," Kyle continued, "I just wanted to say sorry, again, for being so mean to you when I first realized you were here. I...I reacted poorly."

Putting it mildly.

He met her gaze, his eyes earnest. Emma felt her resolve weaken in that moment. This was the old Kyle she had fallen for, kind and sweet.

"Of course," Emma replied gently. "I blindsided you. Completely understandable. No hard feelings."

Like she blindsided him when she asked for a divorce.

A common theme with her, apparently.

Emma cleared her throat, breaking the sudden tension. "So, what's on the agenda for tonight?"

Kyle relaxed, leaning against the counter. "Another movie night?"

He flashed her a crooked grin and Emma felt her knees go weak.

Get it together, you horndog! Her libido was making up for lost time, apparently.

"A movie sounds perfect," she managed.

After she washed up from the day at the stables, they shared a nice dinner then settled onto the couch to fire up the TV. Emma was careful to leave space between them.

Kyle's sandalwood cologne filled her senses, reminding her of late nights spent curled up in his arms. She snuck a glance at his profile, taking in the strong jaw and intense eyes that used to make her melt.

Stop it. The past was done, they were moving on. The end goal was closure and no hatred – certainly not sex or the re-kindling of an old flame.

Her traitorous heart didn't seem to care.

Kyle shifted and Emma realized she'd been staring. Heat flooded her cheeks.

"You okay over there?" He raised an eyebrow.

"Yup, all good!" Emma said brightly, forcing herself to look at the TV.

Kyle chuckled under his breath. The sound sent a pleasant shiver down her spine.

Focus!

But the damage was already done. Being this close to Kyle had cracked open the floodgates, releasing a torrent of buried feelings. And there was no going back now.

Emma tried to keep her eyes on the movie, but her thoughts kept drifting.

She remembered how Kyle used to absently run his fingers through her hair when they watched TV together. The feeling of his strong arms around her, holding her close. The way he'd nuzzle her neck when he was being playful.

God she missed him. Missed them.

Emma glanced over again, taking in Kyle's rugged profile. He looked good. The years had been kind to him.

She wondered suddenly if he was seeing anyone. A flare of jealousy caught her off guard. He had mentioned old girlfriends, but no one currently. Yet, she was curled up in a small chair on the patio last night that still had a pretty perfume smell clinging to it.

In fact, in just the week she'd been there, she'd definitely caught whiffs of it multiple times.

The thought of Kyle with someone else...it hurt. More than she wanted to admit.

Time passed and the movie dragged on. As the credits finally rolled, Emma let out a shaky breath. The living room felt stifling. She needed space to clear her head.

"Well, I'm exhausted. I'll see you in the morning." Her voice sounded overly cheery.

Kyle's eyes searched her face and Emma felt her cheeks growing warm again under his scrutiny.

"Okay. Sleep well," he said, after a moment.

Emma nodded and hurried upstairs before she did something stupid, like throw herself into his arms. She closed her bedroom door firmly behind her and sagged against it.

She had a sinking feeling this was only the beginning. Being around Kyle again had awakened a swarm of feelings she thought were long gone. And she had no idea what to do about it.

Emma took a few deep breaths to calm her racing heart. She could hear Kyle moving around downstairs, closing up the house for the night. The domestic sounds made her ache.

This was the life they were supposed to have together. Instead, she had thrown it all away. And now here they were, two strangers living under one roof.

Emma crossed to the window and looked out at the moonlight filtering through the trees.

With a sigh, she turned away from the window to collapse on the bed.

She had to stay focused. The past was done. All that mattered now was keeping Kyle from finding out the truth, no matter how much it hurt them both.

CHAPTER ELEVEN

October 8, Saturday
Emma

Days later, Emma asked Jen to meet her and Julie at Foals and Fillies.

She needed to talk to someone. Anyone.

Keeping her upcoming medical diagnosis a secret was killing her. Figuratively.

Cancer was the literal killer.

The wait in hearing back from the nurse to schedule the PET scan was torture. She started calling on Wednesday to see if someone could schedule it for her.

No luck.

And she called about the blood work, to which no one was able to answer anything.

She wanted to scream.

So, rather than storming into the hospital and demanding the reports, she called up Jen and Julie and asked for a girls' date.

They jumped at the chance.

Once at Foals and Fillies, Emma took a deep breath, inhaling the familiar scent of hay and horses as she approached the stables. This was one of the few places where she felt truly at peace.

Maybe, if she did have cancer and she was able to beat it...maybe she could buy a horse.

"Emma!" Jen jogged up from behind Emma, her feet pounding on the dirt of the parking lot. "Yeesh, you're so totally deaf. I've been calling your name for ten minutes!"

Emma had been there for two. At most.

She turned and raised her eyebrows to Jen, who just shrugged good naturedly. "It felt like ten minutes. It's okay though, I needed the jog."

"Emma! Jen!" Julie's sweet voice called out to her from the stable doors. Her friend's soft-spoken nature always had a calming effect on Emma. Julie had been the one to introduce her to equine therapies. It was a game changer for her depression after her chemo. Even years later.

"Hey, Julie!" Emma greeted her with a warm smile, embracing her friend in a tight hug. "What a beautiful day for a ride, huh?"

"Absolutely," Julie replied, her eyes shining with excitement. "Just a moment, I have them all geared up and ready for us."

"Here you go, Emma," Julie said, leading Emma's favorite mare, Daisy, out of the stable. The horse nickered softly, flicking its ears in anticipation. Emma couldn't help but feel a rush of adrenaline surge through her veins, as it always did before a ride.

"Thanks, Jules. Hey, pretty baby," Emma murmured, stroking Daisy's velvety muzzle fondly.

"I have yours too, Jen. Hold tight." Julie dashed back into the barn. Only to come out with a pretty, petite, chestnut gelding.

"Ah, Acorn! You're home!" Jen swooped in and started snuggling the old quarter horse. He'd been away at a therapy camp for a week. Jen was his favorite. Hard to believe, given that Jen used to be terrified of horses.

"Ready?" Julie asked, already astride her own horse, a sleek black gelding named Thunder.

"Definitely," Emma replied with determination, swinging herself up into Daisy's saddle.

"Let's ride," Julie said with a grin, urging Thunder forward. Emma followed suit, guiding Daisy out of the stable yard and onto the worn dirt path leading to acres of trails and fields.

"Yee haw!" Jen called out, her brunette ponytail bouncing as she mounted Acorn, and they trotted up the trail beside the others.

"Alrighty then, let's head out," Julie said, leading the way. Emma followed suit, guiding Daisy alongside her friends as they made their way along the trail.

"Have you noticed any improvements with Salsa's leg, Julie?" Emma inquired, asking about a retired racehorse mare that was having some stifle issues a few days ago.

"Definitely," Julie responded enthusiastically. "The meds seem to be working wonders. She's moving so much better now."

"Jen told me about that new hot, new horse vet you found," Emma chimed in. "I heard he gives some good back breaking cracks for you."

Julie gave her an unimpressed look. "He does chiropractic adjustments for the horses. He's yet to touch *my* back."

Jen leaned into Emma from her saddle. "She said 'yet.'" Jen sang out with a teasing lilt.

Emma laughed and whispered loudly to Jen. "I heard that too."

"Brats," Julie pouted, patting Thunder affectionately. "Anyway, it's like she's a whole new horse. So, we'll see how the next two weeks go."

As they rode further along the trail, the trio of friends continued to chat about the horses and life. A gentle breeze rustled through the trees, carrying with it the distant sound of laughter from other riders enjoying the day.

"Isn't it wonderful to see the progress some of these horses have made?" Julie mused, her voice soft and thoughtful. "I've always believed that they have just as much to teach us as we do them."

"Absolutely," Emma agreed, feeling a sense of calm wash over her as she listened to the steady rhythm of Daisy's hooves. "There's something so healing about being around them. No matter how tough things get, I always find solace in their presence."

"Couldn't have said it better myself," Jen chimed in, flashing a knowing grin at her friends. "They say you can lead a horse to water, but you can't make 'em drink. But sometimes, all they need is a little nudge in the right direction."

Emma couldn't help but chuckle at Jen's words, appreciating her friend's unique blend of humor and wisdom.

Emma took a deep breath, inhaling the earthy scent of the dirt beneath them and the sweet aroma of nature. The steady rhythm of Daisy's hooves and the gentle swaying of her gait lulled Emma into a peaceful state, allowing her thoughts to drift.

"Hey, Em," Julie called out, breaking through her reverie. "You seem a bit lost in thought there. Everything okay?"

Emma hesitated, then jumped in, even though she knew it was going to crash their whole happy vibe. "I've just been thinking about Kyle and this whole stalker situation." She bit her lip, the taste of apprehension bitter on her tongue. "It just...sucks."

Julie nodded empathetically; her turquoise blue eyes filled with understanding. "Dude. I seriously don't know how you're getting up in the morning."

"Or sleeping at night," Jen chimed in.

"For sure. I'd be a freaking wreck. I'd never sleep again." Julie tucked a long blonde strand back and wrapped it around her ponytail. Bootstrapping, but efficient.

"I already do, but I'd carry even more mace everywhere. And probably try to go for a concealed carry...if that's even legal here...is it?" Jen's face turned pensive.

The girls looked between them, none of them having the slightest clue about the gun laws in Massachusetts.

"It's just weird. That something so awful brought us...together again. Though together is not quite the right word," Emma mused, tracing a pattern on Daisy's withers with her fingers, more than okay with postponing her cancer confession for another few minutes. "And honestly, when I'm near Kyle, even across the hall from him, the stalker doesn't even cross my mind. Crazy, I know. I should be much more concerned. Yet, somehow, near him...I'm not. Not even a little bit."

"You guys must have had one incredible bond back then for it to translate to today even with all the baggage between you," Julie conceded. "It's heartwarming. That even after heartbreak, there's still a memory there that you and he are honoring and protecting."

Emma wouldn't go that far.

Kyle was pretty freaking angry when he saw her again.

However, he still insisted on her staying with him.

Nerves twirled in her belly.

"I think my stay with him is a blip on our timeline. After his security guy installs my system, I'm out of there and back home. I think it will be better for both of us if we don't look back. Just accept it for what it was: fond memories and maybe a touch of forgiveness."

"Look, Em," Jen said, nudging her horse closer to Emma's. "I know you said that you and Kyle have some baggage, so I'm assuming you're afraid of getting hurt again. But sometimes, you just have to jump back into the game, you know?"

Ah, crap.

Actually, no.

She should do it.

Confess to someone. Anyone.

The silence was strangling her.

"It's not that simple," Emma sighed, her fingers tightening on the reins. "There's...more to it than me being afraid to get hurt."

Jen raised an eyebrow. "Oh, Mrs. Mysterious? Care to explain, finally?"

Emma hesitated, her heart pounding. Finally, she took a deep breath and looked up at the blue sky, her voice barely above a whisper. "When we were in college, I was diagnosed with cancer."

"Emma!" Jen gasped while her eyes widened with shock.

"Yeah-"

"Dios mío, chica! What did he do?" Jen demanded, her concern evident in her tone.

"About that." Emma shifted in her seat which caused Daisy to do a sidestep and toss her head in protest of the moving weight.

Sorry, girl.

"Well...Because he had his football career to focus on, and I didn't want to burden him, I sort of...didn't tell him." Emma admitted, her gaze dropping to Daisy's mane. "He still doesn't know. I just...I just wanted to protect him."

The girls rode in horrified silence next to her.

Crap. It sounded so awful when she said it aloud.

"Emma," Julie said gently, reaching over to touch her arm. "When we met, you said you have been cancer free for a few years. You didn't tell me that you went through it alone."

"Yeah..."

What more was there to say?

What did they want her to say?

"Oh, my God, Emma! You need to tell him!" Jen burst out, nearly vibrating on Acorn. "He needs to know! He'd forgive you in a heartbeat! Actually, he'd probably have this new thing to be mad and broody about, but oh my God, girl!" Jen's voice was high and tense.

Sort of like Emma's nerves at the moment.

"Yeah, no. I absolutely can't tell him." Emma whipped around to face Jen. "And you can't either. No one can. This isn't something he needs to know. He would take on so much guilt and worry. It's already not nice walking back into his life just to leave again." She paused and started again, "Hopefully my departure is not a more...permanent leaving. But in a 'see you later, have a nice life, I wish you nothing but happiness' kind of way."

"No, Jen's right," Julie agreed, her voice soft as usual. "Life is too short to hold onto regrets, Em. If you love him – and I know you do – then, you owe it to both of you to give this a real chance and come clean."

Emma's eyes filled with tears as she absorbed her friends' advice. If only they were right.

"There's something else."

"Let me guess, in the meantime you had his secret baby?"

Emma gave Jen an unenthusiastic look. "No. Brat." She took a deep breath. "I can't tell him because I think the cancer is back."

Both of her friends turned to her in their saddles, their mouths open in shock and horror. For several footfalls, there was nothing but the sound of swishing horse tails and Thunder chewing on his bit.

After a beat of the girls processing her declaration, both of them started peppering her with questions.

"Back? Why do you think that? Is that why you were at the hospital?" Jen asked, her Latina accent getting thicker.

"Are you sure? Have you seen a doctor or gotten checked out?" Julie demanded.

Emma shook her head, patting Daisy reassuringly when the mare tossed her head.

Did Julie remember to wipe her ears with bug spray before they headed out?

"Yeah, I've seen a doctor. I'm having the same symptoms as before. But the *coup de Grâce*, is the lump in my right breast. My first round of blood work was a little out of normal range. I'm still waiting for the second round's results. *And* I'm waiting for them to *freaking schedule me a freaking scan*!" Emma ended on a shout that caused Daisy's ears to flit backward to her. "But no one will return my call and I don't know what to do!" She transitioned into a sob that had Julie pulling the group to a stop and dismounting, rounding her way to Emma's left side, and helping her to slide off Daisy. Jen followed suit and rounded Acorn. She went into Julie's saddle bags and started digging for tissues.

"Hey now, it's going to be okay, Ems. It might not even be back, and if it is, we'll fight it. You of all people know that cancer isn't an automatic death sentence. We got this," Julie soothed, rubbing Emma's shoulders and accepting the tissues Jen handed her, passing them to Emma.

"We'll visit their offices daily until they schedule your PET scan and damnit, if the results come back positive, we'll be at every treatment with water guns and jokes." Jen promised. "We'll shave our heads in solidarity. And you know how much I love my hair."

Emma sniffled and dabbed at her eyes and nose, giggling wetly. Daisy nudged Julie's shoulder, snuffling her ear and making her laugh and push her head away.

"Daisy agrees." Julie said, giving the mare a scratch. Emma managed a watery smile, putting the used tissues into her pocket and snagging Jen and Julie for a three-way hug.

"Thank you guys." She said in a watery voice.

"Don't get snot on me. I only deal with horse snot, not people snot. People snot is gross." Julie tried pulling away with a chuckle and Emma turned and wiped her face, snot and all, all over Julie's shirt.

The girls burst into giggles and stepped away, taking big breaths as they looked at each other.

"Em...honey. I don't know what to say." Jen wiped at her tears.

"You don't have to say anything. You're just here. That's enough."

They gave each other watery smiles.

"Not to harp on the matter, but you really aren't going to tell Kyle?" Jen's face was concerned and clearly questioning the wisdom of that decision.

"Would you? Would you burden John like that if it were you?"

Jen blinked and cocked her head. "Of course, I'd tell John. He's my rock, my best friend, my heart. I can't imagine facing something like that without him. And he'd be furious if I didn't tell him. Have you seen John mad? He's impressively terrifying. I can't imagine what he'd do if he found out I had cancer and didn't tell him..." Jen trailed off. "Actually, you're right. Don't tell him. If he was arrested for murder, our team would lose our fullback and we don't have the reserves to replace his position on the field."

Julie smacked Jen on the arm. "Shut up." She then turned to Emma, her worried face made her two dimples even more pronounced. "Em, you don't need to decide right now. But he deserved to know then, to have a say in whether he wanted to stick around. Just like he deserves a say now. Don't take his agency from him."

"He would have stuck around." Emma whispered out. "That was the problem. And he wouldn't have had his dreams come true."

"Honey, from what you've said during all our chats over the last two weeks, that guy's dreams centered around you."

Julie hit that square on the head.

She had no idea how right she was.

"Okay," Emma whispered, swallowing hard and wiping away a stray tear. "I'll think about it. I just...need some time."

Giving Emma's hand a reassuring squeeze, Julie said, "We're here for you, no matter what."

"Damn straight," Jen chimed in, flashing a cheeky grin. "And if that hunky football player breaks your heart, well...I know where his pain points are and I can make him *feel* them, if you know what I mean." Being their massage and pre-hab therapist...Jen wasn't joking.

Their soft chuckles rippled through the air, a gentle testament of companionship that echoed over the fields.

As they got back on their horses and started back up on their ride, Emma's heart felt lighter than it had in ages.

That was it.

It was over.

The secret was done.

She shared.

And, man, it felt so good.

A weight was finally lifted from her shoulders.

A burden released.

More freedom.

Just in time to face death.

Emma jerked from her morbid thoughts as Jen laughed randomly next to her.

"It just goes to show," Jen chimed in, her mischievous half grin appearing as quickly as it vanished. "You never know when a handsome football player might come galloping back into your life, solving all your problems and restoring your faith in life and love."

"Dork" Emma laughed, swiping at her friend as a chuckle slipped out of her.

"Hey, I'm just saying," Jen shrugged, her eyes twinkling with mirth. "Sometimes, the heart knows what it wants, even if our heads try to convince us otherwise."

"This is sage advice coming from you, of all people." Julie chimed in, her eyes twinkling.

"Yeah, I know. I've matured since not hanging out with Lexie as much." Jen laughed hard at that. "Anyway, what we need now is a good old-fashioned distraction. So – first one to that big oak tree up ahead gets to pick our next book club read, and, if I win, I'm choosing one of Emma's steamy romances!"

"Jen, you're such a turd," Emma laughed, her spirits lifting despite the turmoil roiling within her.

"What I didn't hear was a 'no.'" Jen pushed, her feisty eyes blazing.

Julie's horse broke stride first. He flew forward but only got a length ahead before Emma and Jen followed in swift pursuit.

With a chorus of laughter and playful jeers, the trio urged their horses into a gallop, the wind whipping through their hair as they raced toward the finish line. Emma's heart pounded in exhilaration, the thrill of the chase momentarily pushing her fears about Kyle and her past diagnosis to the back of her mind.

However, as they made their way back to Foals and Fillies, Emma's thoughts once again strayed to Kyle. She couldn't shake the nagging feeling that telling him about her diagnosis from years ago might only push him further away – or worse, make him feel obligated to stay with her now out of pity. The thought of burdening him with her illness, especially when she didn't have her latest results back, felt like a betrayal in itself.

CHAPTER TWELVE

October 9, Sunday
Kyle

The locker room buzzed with post-game adrenaline and the air thick and humid from their collective sweat. Kyle, his muscles tired and aching, collapsed onto a bench, gripping a towel around his neck as he sought the counsel of his teammates.

"Guys, I need your advice about Emma," he blurted out, feeling the weight of his unresolved feelings pressing down on him.

One of their safeties was the first to weigh in. "Kyle, my man, just hit it and quit it!" He laughed boisterously, slapping Kyle's shoulder a bit too hard.

"Thanks for the sage wisdom," Kyle muttered sarcastically under his breath, rolling his eyes at the predictability of his teammate's response. As much as he appreciated the camaraderie of his fellow athletes, their insights into matters of the heart often left something to be desired.

Hence why he was directing his question to the more emotionally stable teammates: Kenny, Brandon, Danny, Liam, Michael, Kobe, heck, even the Golden Boy, Ryan.

"Look, Kyle," Michael started, "I know you said things are going smoother at home. But I gotta tell you, don't let the past hold you back. Especially if this stalker thing develops further. What if she got hurt – would you be able to forgive yourself for not trying to see things through?"

Kyle sighed heavily, rubbing his hand over his face, feeling the grit and sweat clinging to his skin. He'd shower after he got some fucking guidance on how to feel and what to do.

His mind tumbled through memories of late nights tangled in bedsheets and whispered promises that seemed as distant as the stars. The distrust he still harbored toward Emma clawed at his chest, a constant reminder of their past. And yet, when she was near, that magnetic pull only intensified, an electric current humming beneath his skin.

"Are you sure it's worth it, though?" Kyle asked, his voice wavering slightly. "I mean, she wrecked me once. What's stopping her from doing it again?"

"Kyle, buddy, you can't live your life in fear of what might happen," Danny chimed. "You'll just end up stuck and miserable."

'Stuck and miserable' was a pretty accurate description of how Kyle felt at that moment, torn between his lingering anger and the undeniable attraction that flared every time he locked eyes with those precious periwinkle blues.

He clenched and unclenched his fists, trying to force the conflicting emotions into some semblance of order.

No dice.

"Maybe you're right," he conceded, his voice quiet in comparison to the riot of conversations bouncing around the locker room. "I don't know. It's just...hard, you know?"

His buddies nodded solemnly, their eyes filled with empathy and understanding. They had all faced their own battles, both on and off the field.

"Whatever you decide, man," said Liam, "We got you. At least it's not life or death."

"Sure can feel like it sometimes." Kenny mumbled. Michael gave a hum of agreement.

"Thanks," Kyle murmured, feeling a small measure of relief in knowing he wasn't alone in his struggle.

All that said, he didn't have a damn clue as to which path to choose.

Danny clapped him on the shoulder. "Come on, man, you never know what might happen if you give her a chance," he said through a grin. "Maybe she had a good reason all those years ago."

"Or maybe she hasn't changed at all, and it'll just be a repeat of last time," countered Brandon, while folding his massive arms across his chest. The skeptical offensive lineman had a habit of seeing the darker side of things, and right now, that didn't exactly help Kyle's state of mind.

"Guys, all that's well and good because we all *think* we know Emma," Liam said, glancing around at the other guys. "But clearly there's a side to her that we don't know. And for reasons we don't know, she already wrecked our man once. So, maybe he doesn't jump right in and makes her work for it. See how much she's willing to work for it. You don't want to end up hurt again, do you?"

Kyle shook his head, frustration mounting. It seemed as if everyone had an opinion, but none of them offered any real clarity. He glanced around the room, taking in the sea of concerned faces. All except for one – Ryan Cole. The quarterback had remained silent throughout the entire discussion, his eyes locked on Kyle with an intensity that was borderline unnerving.

"All right, man, you've been quiet this whole time," Kyle finally addressed Ryan, unable to ignore the penetrating sapphire gaze any longer. "Lay it on me."

Ryan hesitated for a moment before speaking, his voice low and measured. "I know Emma outside of all this...football stuff," he began. "We go riding horses together at Julie's—"

"So you've said about a thousand fucking times. I get it. You guys had a 'thing.' Move on. She's not yours to keep playing with."

Kyle was going to fucking strangle Ryan if he kept bringing it up.

Acting like he knew Emma better than Kyle did.

It was fucking ridiculous and downright false.

No one knew her better than he did.

And while he liked Ryan, he'd be a terrible partner for Emma.

Just the thought made him want to tackle the guy through the wall and break a few of his most important bones. Instead, Kyle settled for grinding his teeth, popping his neck, and cracking his knuckles.

It didn't cool the edge.

"It wasn't like that," Ryan protested, holding up his hands defensively. "We talk, we ride horses together. That's all. We're friends." Then the younger man paused and added stupidly, "She is gorgeous and great, though, isn't she?"

That's it, Kyle was going to break Ryan's finger at practice this week.

Whoops, sorry kid. Bumped you a little too rough there. My bad.

"Except it's not 'all', is it?" Kyle shot back, feeling the familiar heat of indignation rising within him. "Because now you're here, acting like you know her better than I do."

Ryan leveled Kyle with a stern gaze, his voice firm as he spoke. "I'm just saying, don't break her heart again, all right? Mickey's got a guy that I could call in a heartbeat – and I'd lose no sleep. That woman has hurt a mile deep in her eyes. I don't know what happened then or now, I just know that she shouldn't have to handle any more of it. So, save me from having to put a hit out on you, will ya?"

Kyle bristled and the other guys grew quiet. "What the fuck does that mean?"

"It means don't break her heart. It's been through enough."

"Break her heart?" Kyle scoffed, incredulous. "Yeah, right. Were you not listening? She broke mine. What kind of lies has she been feeding you?"

"Kyle, I'm not saying you did anything wrong," Ryan replied, his expression softening slightly. "But whatever happened between you two back then, it's clear there's more to the story. Don't let your past dictate your future without at least trying to understand her side of things."

Well, that didn't sound like it was coming from a man who had a romantic interest in his wife. Ex-wife. Fuck, old habits died hard.

When he saw 'Potter' plastered on the side of her mailbox when he went snooping on her house, he wanted to punch a hole through his window. Then she came flying out and almost got herself run over. The rest was history.

His body loosened the barest amount. She was living with him and she'd mentioned Ryan only in passing – there was no way they were dating. If she was being honest to the police officers that took her statement a few weeks ago...there was no dating at all.

Suspicious...but a relief, nonetheless.

Blood flow returned to his brain and he took a deep breath to get control again.

Fuck, he was unstable.

Emma made him unstable.

As much as Kyle wanted to dismiss Ryan's words, something in his gut told him that his friend might be right.

Had he been so blinded by his own pain that he'd never truly tried to understand Emma's perspective?

The thought gnawed at him, upsetting the comfortable narrative he'd clung to for years.

"Fine," he muttered begrudgingly, feeling both indignant and confused. "I'll talk to her, try to get to the bottom of this."

"Just keep an open mind, all right? You don't know where her head's at until you talk it out. Regardless, she's not the person you remember," Ryan stated, his tone almost pleading. "The person she is today...she'd never yank the rug out from you like that. No way. She'd talk it out first. Explain her side of things. So, I think you need to see her for who she is now, not who she was back then."

The kid made it sound so simple.

When it just wasn't.

All these years, he had been clinging to a version of her in his head. A ghost of a memory.

And now he was hearing that version of Emma no longer existed?

"How can you be so sure? You didn't even know her then."

"No. But I know her now," Ryan assured Kyle. "And that'd be enough for me and I gotta tell you, man. You wait too long, someone else will take their shot. And you'll be left holding nothing but a dusty divorce certificate."

Was Ryan suggesting *he* was going to be that 'someone else?'

Kyle was again struck with the urge to slam the kid's head through a table, full on WWE style.

But Ryan's expression was earnest, not threatening. Pleading.

Like he was on 'Team Kymma.'

Kyle took a deep breath and thought about Ryan's words. They felt...right.

He was so busy trying to cling to the Emma he used to know, that he overlooked the Emma she was today. How much more had she changed?

Surprisingly...he wanted to find out.

And wasn't that telling.

Kyle felt a spark of hope ignite in his chest.

Perhaps it was time to confront the past head-on – and finally discover who this new Emma Potter truly was.

As Kyle drove home after the game, his mind was consumed with different scenarios.

What happened, back before his draft that caused their abrupt breakup?

Did someone threaten her?

Did someone in town say something that was the final straw?

Did a coach or teammate approach her, causing her to run?

Ultimately, it all boiled down to: was there more to Emma's story than he had been willing to entertain?

As he drove home, Kyle's perspective on Emma began to evolve. He questioned the assumptions he'd made and considered the possibility of a different truth – a truth that might change everything between them. His heart raced at the thought with equal parts excitement and dread.

What could it have been?

She clearly had loved him.

Still did, if her constant staring and shy, tentative smiles were anything to go by.

As he waited at a red light, he looked up into the rearview mirror.

"All right, Emma," he said to his reflection, taking a deep breath. "It's time to find out who you really are."

Whatever truth lay ahead, he would face it head-on, even if it meant reevaluating everything he thought he knew about the woman he'd once loved. And maybe they could find their way back to each other again – or at least, find closure on a chapter that had remained open ended for far too long.

It was time to have a heart-to-heart with his ex-wife. What could possibly go wrong?

CHAPTER THIRTEEN

October 10, Monday
Emma

The car's engine hummed as Emma and Kyle cruised down the highway, the Springfield skyline fading in their rearview mirror. The tension in the air was tangible.

"All right, what about that guy from the gym?" Emma asked, tapping her fingers on her thigh. "He was definitely watching me."

Kyle growled in agreement, his hands tightening on the steering wheel. "He certainly was."

"He didn't really look like the type to read thrillers though," Emma conceded, glancing out the window. "But we can't rule anyone out. This whole situation is just so...bizarre. There was that guy from Victor's last week. The one we saw two nights in a row?"

"Yeah, he was looking at you, too," Kyle grumbled, his eyes narrowing as he focused on the road. They lapsed into an uneasy silence, their brains going in wildly different directions.

"Or maybe it was that woman from the grocery store after the gym! She kept telling me how much she loved my outfit..."

"Yeah, it couldn't possibly have been the brain-melting outfit you had on. It was practically a second skin. I think the guy at the gym was practicing his breathing techniques because he didn't need much imagin—"

She hit his arm and laughed. "Oh, shut it. It wasn't that bad."

"Talk to me when you're a guy..."

She elbowed him, genial but corrective. Then blurted out, "Oh! Do you remember in college when we snuck into the football stadium the night before homecoming?" She looked over at Kyle, a nostalgic smile tugging at the corners of her lips. "That security guard certainly caught a show. It could have been him."

Kyle chuckled, shaking his head. "Yeah, and you climbed up onto the field goal post like some kind of daredevil. I still don't know what possessed you. You were always so cautious; it was wicked out of character..."

"Hey, in my defense, I had to show you that you didn't just marry some boring bookworm," she shot back playfully, her blue eyes sparkling with mischief.

"I never thought you were boring," he admitted, the corner of his mouth lifting into a half-smile. He glanced at her before returning his gaze to the road, as the memories came flooding back. "You were always full of surprises."

"Like that time we took that weekend trip to the beach," Emma continued, her mind drifting back to happier times. "I'll never forget how furious you were when I buried your clothes in the sand while you were in the water."

"You're lucky I found them, or I would've had to walk back to the hotel naked," Kyle laughed, the tension in his shoulders easing slightly. "Or steal something from you."

"It wouldn't have been the worst view," Emma teased, her cheeks flushing a light pink. She bit her lip and looked away, suddenly aware of the charged atmosphere between them. "You squeezing into my pink sarong would have been cute. I doubt you'd fit into it now."

He'd certainly filled out since college.

Kyle's laughter faded. "Those were good times, weren't they?"

"Really good times," she agreed with a wistful nod, her heart aching with the bittersweet memories. They had been so young and in love once, their future full of endless possibilities. But life had a way of complicating things, and now they sat in a car together, driving towards the police station so she could look at mugshots of people that might want to hurt her. If they caught the person who had ransacked her home, she'd have no reason to stay with Kyle. She'd be out of his life. Forever.

Unless…

"Hey," he began hesitantly, "I've been meaning to ask you about your writing career. You're kind of a big deal now. How does it feel knowing that you finally made it?"

Emma chuckled and waved his praise away. "I'm not sure if I could technically say that I've 'made it.' I still have down months. You should see me when the numbers start dropping. I look like a freaking investigator as I try to pinpoint what caused the drop in sales. The only thing missing is a magnifying glass."

He chuckled, just as she hoped he would. "What is it usually?

"The eternal question. There's never a set rhyme or reason. Tropes and genres come and go. Hockey romance was hot, then it was billionaires, then it was romantic fantasy, then it was rom coms. So, it could just be a genre swing. It could be an influencer or marketing push. Could be a pricing shift, or maybe my covers fell out of style. Any number of things.

Emma was touched by his genuine curiosity. She loved talking shop.

Kyle shifted in his seat and a funny look came over his face as he admitted, "I sort of snooped and looked you up. Chloe gave me your pen names. You seem to have a lot of good reviews." Emma nodded, waiting for his question. "But what the hell does being indie mean?"

She chuckled. "Well, when my stuff is traditionally published it means I have a contract with a publishing house who handles editing, cover design, marketing, and getting the books into stores. Being indie means I do all that myself or hire freelance contractors to help. It gives me more control and flexibility, but it can also be a lot more work. It depends on the book."

He pursed his lips to the side. "I don't remember you talking about self-publishing in college."

"It's gotten a lot more popular in recent years. There are a lot of big names that self-publish now. It's been an incredible journey, and the industry has changed so much since I started. There are more opportunities for authors now, but it's also incredibly competitive."

"Sounds like professional football," Kyle chuckled, shooting her a quick grin. "You know what my days are like, but I really have no idea what you do all day after I head into the stadium. What's it like?"

"Every day is different, but typically I start my mornings with emails and marketing, then get some writing in before lunch." Emma paused, her eyes twinkling with mischief. "And then, of course, I spend the afternoon lounging around in silk pajamas, eating Nutella by the spoonful, and dictating my next masterpiece to my team of loyal, sexy scribes."

"Ah, the glamorous life of a bestselling author," Kyle laughed, playing along. "You're living your dream, Em," Kyle said sincerely. He glanced over at her, his eyes lingering on her face. "I'm happy for you."

Her cheeks warmed at his compliment, and she looked out the window to hide her sudden shyness. "Thank you, Kyle," she murmured, feeling a mix of gratitude and vulnerability.

"Not to change the subject," Kyle began, a teasing glint in his eyes as he made a turn at a light. "But I've noticed that some of the books are…quite steamy."

Emma's cheeks felt like they were on fire. "My romance novels? Yeah, they can get a little…intense at times."

"Intense, huh?" Kyle smiled outright, unable to hide his amusement. "I found some passages shared online. Emma, Emma, Emma. What would your grandmother say?" His laugh made her stomach tighten in the most delectable way. This was the Kyle she remembered.

"Hey, what can I say?" She worked through the embarrassment his teasing invoked. "People seem to enjoy them. They sell well."

"Is that how you come up with those hot scenes?" Kyle asked, his voice dropped into a deeper note. "By imagining what people might enjoy?"

A shudder of forbidden excitement raced through her.

"Something like that," Emma mumbled, avoiding his gaze as she fiddled with the hem of her shirt. The thought of Kyle reading her most private scenes inspired a wave of flutters deep in her belly.

Even though some of the sex scenes weren't her cup of tea at all, there was a market for variety, so she kept her scenes as fresh and imaginative as possible. Even if she herself had never, nor would ever, participate in such acts. Even so, some of those puppies were *fire*.

"Must be fun, getting paid to write about passion and desire," he commented, still in that low, sexy tone. "Do you ever feel like you're living vicariously through your characters?"

"Sometimes," she admitted, her heart pounding in her chest as she dared to meet his eyes. "But there's nothing wrong with a bit of harmless escapism, right?"

"Of course not," Kyle agreed, his face softening. "Besides, I can see why you'd be good at it. You always had a way with words."

"Just not speaking them?"

He grinned as he took another turn. "You weren't the *best* speaker, that's for sure."

"Public speaking still gives me hives."

His bright white teeth flashed under his black closely trimmed beard. "That's my girl. Consistent as the tide."

"Oh, God. Remember that night at Hampton Beach?" Emma couldn't help but smile at the memory. "That riptide was wicked intense. I thought I was going to drown!"

"I told you not to go out there. Thank God I was able to get to you. I wasn't too disappointed with how you thanked me after, if I remember correctly, " Kyle said with a wistful sigh. There was silence for a beat. "We had some good times, didn't we?"

"More than good," Emma murmured, glancing out the window.

As they continued their slow drive through crazy construction traffic, the car seemed to grow warmer, the air between them thick with tension and unspoken desires. Emma couldn't help but notice how Kyle's strong hands gripped the steering wheel, the way his muscles flexed beneath his shirt, the scent of his cologne – it was all so familiar, yet undeniably enticing.

"Maybe I should try my hand at writing one of those steamy scenes," Kyle mused, his voice low and teasing. "I bet I could give you a run for your money."

"Is that a challenge?" Emma asked as she raised an eyebrow.

"Maybe it is," he replied, his gaze never leaving hers. "Just imagine what we could come up with together…"

For a moment, time seemed to stand still as they locked eyes, the air crackling with electricity. But then Emma blinked, breaking the spell, and they both laughed nervously, trying to dispel the sudden intensity of their connection.

Which was good, because the guy was driving a freaking car and needed to keep his eyes on the road!

"Let's just stick to solving this investigation for now," Emma suggested, her voice slightly breathless. "One step at a time, right?"

"Right," Kyle agreed, his dark eyes still smoldering with unspoken desire. "One step at a time."

Emma looked out the window, her fingers drumming against her thigh. She couldn't deny the spark that was beginning to smolder, but she knew they needed to tread carefully.

At one point during their drive, he had reached over and tucked a stray curl behind her ear. She had thought she was going to pass out from that one small gesture.

Their earlier flirtation had opened a door that neither could fully close, and now they stood on the precipice of something deeper, something more intense.

"We're here. Finally." Kyle pulled into a spot at the police station and threw the car in park. "We need a few more roundabouts to lessen our dependence on stop lights because holy hell, *that* was torture. *One* intersection loses power, and all hell breaks loose. Hopefully they don't mind that we're a bit late."

Emma couldn't find anything to say. It was so...domestic...his comments. His behavior. His attitude. He was her Kyle again.

For a heartbeat, they simply stared at one another, the world outside their car fading away. They were just Emma and Kyle, two people with a complicated history and an undeniable connection. But as quickly as it had come, the moment passed. "We should probably head in," Kyle said quietly, his voice thick with unspoken emotion.

"Right," Emma replied, her heart racing in her chest. "Let's go."

As they stepped out of the car, she couldn't help but wonder what the future held for them, especially if they walked out of there today with some viable suspects.

Why did that possibility fill her with such disappointment?

CHAPTER FOURTEEN

October 10, Monday
Emma

Emma slammed the car door, grinding her teeth together as she followed Kyle up the walkway to his house.

That was such a waste of time!

"Can you believe those guys?" Emma huffed. "It's like they're not even trying."

"Trust me, I know," Kyle grumbled, fumbling with his keys. "It's fine. We'll get there. My guy should be able to stop by this week or next to install his system. You'll be good. And then we'll catch the fucker on camera and nail him to the fucking wall."

The moment they stepped inside the house, Emma noticed something was off. Kyle's house alarm was turned off, which was unusual enough, but the interior was spotless – the kind of clean that made you think twice about sitting on the furniture. She glanced around, suppressing a shiver of unease.

"Kyle, did you hire a cleaning service or something?" she asked, her voice tight with nerves.

He shook his head, his near-black eyes scanning the room with a furrowed brow. "No, I didn't. This...isn't right."

"Is this like a hazing thing the guys on the teams do? Make the rookies clean the veterans' houses?"

"Shh." His eyes were scanning and he reached out to grab her hand.

Shh? Why 'shh'?

"Someone broke in?" Emma suggested hesitantly, her mind racing with possibilities.

It was hard to imagine a burglar taking the time to tidy up after themselves, but stranger things had happened.

"Let's just...look around," Kyle said, his voice low and cautious.

Look around? This is how her characters were ambushed in her thrillers!

They needed to call the freaking police!

Instead, she bit her tongue. Maybe Kyle's teammates were just trying a jump scare.

Douche move, given the climate swirling around her right now.

But better than the alternative.

That someone was *here*.

She couldn't believe this was happening again.

As they ventured further into the immaculate living space, Emma shivered.

This was wrong. And stupid.

What wasn't wrong was how handsome Kyle looked when he was in defensive mode.

"Whoever did this has a serious obsession with organization," she quipped, trying to inject some humor into the tense situation. "I mean, who alphabetizes a spice rack?" She pulled her eyes from the corner shelf in the kitchen and continued to inspect the house with him.

Kyle managed a brief smile, the corners of his eyes crinkling. "I don't know, but I'm half-tempted to keep them on retainer."

"Seriously though," Emma continued, her voice dropping to a whisper as they approached the office space. "What do you think is going on? This doesn't feel like a random break-in."

"I don't know," Kyle admitted, giving her hand a reassuring squeeze. "But we'll figure it out, I promise."

The office was completely scrubbed and sanitized.

They cautiously made their way to the living room.

"Do we call the cops?" Emma glanced around the space, the situation weighing heavily on her. The lingering scent of lemon cleaning solution permeated the air, only adding to the eerie atmosphere. She turned to Kyle, searching his face for answers. "Kyle, do you need to call around? Ask any of the guys if they know who did this?"

"Emma, I don't think it was the guys," he replied cautiously, concern etched on his face.

He clearly didn't want to alarm her, but his unease was obvious.

His grip on her hand tightened as they continued through the house.

"We should call the police," she suggested again, her voice wavering slightly.

"Let's just go through the rest of the house first and see if anything is missing."

What if they stumbled into the person who'd done this?

She didn't love that plan – but okay.

Kyle kept Emma close as they moved from room to room. Every surface gleamed, even the usually cluttered countertops in the kitchen.

It was unsettling, to say the least.

"Check this out," Kyle whispered, gesturing toward the security system by the front door. Emma had already noted that, but apparently he hadn't.

The alarm had been disarmed, its green light now replaced with a blinking red one. He quickly reset it, the familiar beep echoing through the otherwise silent house. "Why would someone break in, clean up, then leave the alarm off?"

"Maybe they wanted us to feel freaked?" Emma voiced an obvious guess, pressing closer to Kyle while she glanced over her shoulder. "Or maybe they're trying to send a message."

"Either way," Kyle murmured. "I don't like it."

"Neither do I." Her gaze flickered back to Kyle, noting the tension in his jaw and the furrow of his brow. She couldn't deny she felt safer with him by her side.

As they reached the top of the stairs, Kyle turned to Emma and whispered, "Stay close, okay?"

"Trust me, I'm not going anywhere," she replied, her voice laced with a hint of sarcasm despite her fear. The absurdity of the situation almost made her want to laugh.

Together, they searched each room, looking for any signs of intrusion or tampering. But all they found was more immaculate order as if someone had taken great care to arrange everything just so.

The sight of her perfectly fluffed pillows and crisp, fresh linens only heightened her anxiety.

"All right, we've searched everywhere," Kyle said, taking a deep and steadying breath. "There's no sign that whoever did this is still here."

"This is really weird, by the way," Emma felt compelled to add.

"Agreed," he conceded. "Let's give the detectives a call so they can come by and check things out. But I'm not so sure what they're going to find."

Especially now that Kyle had traipsed through the whole thing, dragging her along and contaminating any evidence that might have been left behind.

Kyle probably wouldn't appreciate hearing that, though.

"While we wait for them to show up, I'm going to update the system to a new code, ask my buddy if anything funky registered in his remote detection system, and shut the curtains."

Emma nodded and chewed on her lower lip.

Was staying here the right call?

Her gut was telling her to leave. Immediately.

"Let's order some food and watch a movie while we wait for them," Kyle suggested gently. "We both need a distraction from all this stress."

"Who knew that a clean house would be so traumatic, huh?" Emma teased, weakly, her nerves finally catching up to her.

She did this. If she hadn't come here, he never would have been violated like this.

"Kyle, I...I'm sorry," she blurted out, her voice thick with emotion. "For everything that's happening now. For everything that happened between us in the past. I know I hurt you, and, and...I'm still managing to hurt you. I never wanted that."

"Emma," he began, his expression softening as he reached out to touch her arm. "None of this is your fault. And..." he took a heaving breath. "And people get divorced. It sucks, but it's not like you weren't allowed to do what you needed to do. I'm...trying to be more accepting of that. But this, here? None of this is your fault."

"Thank you," she whispered, trying to hold back the tears burning her eyes.

"Come on," Kyle said, guiding her towards the living room. "Let's find something to watch and take our minds off all this sketchy-ass cleanliness. I think I still have some laundry I can strew about if that makes you feel better."

She gave him a wet chuckle, but otherwise let herself be pushed down onto the couch.

Again, should they still be here? Were they contaminating the scene?

Kyle handed her the remote and walked back into the kitchen to place his calls.

After a few minutes, he came back and Emma pushed play on the movie she'd chosen.

"Thank you," she murmured.

"Hey," Kyle said softly, drawing her gaze back up to his face. "We're good. It's good. Breathe easy."

"Still," she replied, swallowing hard against the lump in her throat. "It means a lot to me."

For the first time in a lifetime, as they settled into the couch, Kyle sat next to her.

Their bodies naturally gravitated closer together, their shoulders touching and the heat from his body warming her skin.

It felt like an unspoken agreement, a silent promise that they were there for each other, come what may.

Kyle shifted a little bit away and her heart fell.

Oh.

When he reached down and gently lifted one of Emma's feet onto his lap, his warm hands beginning to massage her foot with tender care, Emma's heart fluttered madly in her chest. Sucking in deep shaky breaths didn't help at all. The intimacy of the gesture caught her off guard, sending a quiver down her spine and momentarily easing her anxiety in one way, and ramping it up in another.

"Is this okay?" He asked, his deep eyes searching hers.

"Yeah," she breathed, nodding her head slightly. "It feels...nice."

"Good," he murmured, his attention shifting back to the movie as he continued to rub her foot, his strong fingers working out the knots and tension that had built up throughout the stressful day.

How was she supposed to focus on anything but the warmth of Kyle's touch and the steady rhythm of his breaths?

The police eventually arrived and Kyle paused the movie. Taking her hand, he pulled her up from the couch and they met the officers at the door. Explaining to them that the house was unnervingly clean felt awkward but given the stalker situation swirling around them...it felt right to at least get it on record and see if the police could find anything they missed.

Hand in hand, Kyle pulled Emma around as he pointed out various discrepancies to the police...who, honestly, seemed more starstruck by meeting Kyle than they were concerned for clean criminal that had invaded his home.

Emma gritted her teeth as the officers mixed in football anecdotes while asking their questions and giving precursory views of the moved items. They didn't even pull out a fingerprinting kit.

Weren't they supposed to be dusting for fingerprints or something?

They weren't taking this seriously at all!

This was further proven after they made their way back to the front door and the cops leveled Kyle with a teasing and admiring look. "Definitely think it was one of the guys on the team just messing with you, Justice. With nothing being stolen, no threats, no sign of forced entry – we have nothing to go on besides maybe a prankster on your team that has poor timing." They leaned forward conspiratorially, "Maybe it was Polowski? Or Dillon?" A half shrug later and then they lost all semblance of professionalism as they asked, "Before we go, can we get a picture and an autograph?"

Bless his heart. Kyle quickly covered the rage that had begun to tighten his frame and cause his hand to flex tightly on hers. But like the good sports idol he was, he put on a friendly mask and posed for the pictures.

Though, he didn't smile for them.

His popularity must feel like such an intrusion, especially in moments like these. Emma's heart went out to him, and she gave him a soft smile of support when he turned to catch her eye.

After Kyle firmly closed the door behind the police officers, he leveled Emma with a tired look. "Well, we didn't get the A Team tonight."

She gave him a wry smile but otherwise didn't comment. He knew they got the shit end of the available officers on duty. Then again, calling to report that Kyle's house was 'too clean' was probably odd – but given his connection to her and her stalker, she thought that the police would have taken it more seriously...

"I'll make some calls in the morning. See if any of the guys fess up to pulling a prank. Then I'll see about connecting with someone else on the force. See if they can come by and at least give things a second look." He heaved a big sigh and wiped his face with his hand before giving her a soft look. "But we're fine, so let's just go back to our movie, try to relax, and tackle tomorrow...tomorrow."

Once again, he held her hand as he escorted her back to the couch. Kyle then immediately resumed his position at her feet, continuing his comforting massage from earlier.

He got up quickly when the food finally showed up, an hour late, but otherwise he didn't move from his comforting position.

This. This was her Kyle.

The rest of the night continued in companionable silence.

As the final credits rolled across the screen, Kyle hit the mute button on the remote and turned to face Emma. The room was illuminated only by the glow of the television, casting a soft light on their faces.

"Emma," he began cautiously, his voice a quiet rumble in the dimly lit room. "I know we've both made shitty decisions, but I want to stress to you that I'm here for you now. With this stalker shit. I know I said it earlier, but I want to say it again. I'm trying to move on from...what happened to us. Trying to move past it. Someday I hope you'll explain why you left, but until you're ready...I'm here. I'm...always here."

Emma stared into his eyes, wanting nothing more than to wrap her arms around him and never let go.

Ugh! She wished she at least had her diagnosis already so she could have some honest conversations with him. She didn't want to give him a half picture and then another half picture later. It had to be a band aid removal. All at once.

Crap.

She bit her lip, considering his words before she spoke. "Kyle, I never wanted to hurt you. There was just a lot going on back then, and I didn't know how to handle everything that was happening. I didn't want to be a distraction to you and truly felt like leaving was the only viable option. I can't...I can't..." She swallowed and changed what she was going to say. "I promise you honesty from here on out but I just can't really talk about what happened yet. I'm just not ready."

He watched her closely, noticing the way her fingers nervously twisted a loose thread on the couch cushion. "Okay," he said softly. "Honesty from here on out. Deal."

"Still," she continued, her voice barely above a whisper, "I wish I hadn't pushed you away like I did. I know it doesn't change anything, but I *am* sorry."

Kyle reached out, his fingers gently brushing against her hand, causing a shiver to run down her spine. "Apology accepted," he murmured, his eyes filled with warmth.

"Thank you, Kyle," Emma whispered, feeling a lone tear drip down her cheek. "For being patient with me, for protecting me, and for just...being here."

"Always, Emma," he replied, his voice thick with emotion. "I'll always be here for you."

Till death do us part.

And man, what a jerk that made her, that she was seriously going to bring him down with her. If she was merciful, she'd leave. Now. Before either of them got in any deeper. Instead, here she was, setting her feet in the drying concrete and refusing to budge.

Forgive me, Kyle, she asked of him in a silent prayer.

As the night drew to a close, they reluctantly untangled themselves from each other, and went to their rooms. They stood in the hallway, their hands still linked.

"Goodnight, Emma," Kyle said in a tentative whisper, his eyes searching hers.

"Goodnight, Kyle," she returned, her own octave matching his.

With a final squeeze of their joined hands, they parted ways, each retreating to their own space.

As Emma silently cried in her pillow, she couldn't stop the self-hate from blooming anew.

Why wasn't she strong enough to save him this time? Why was she so selfish?

CHAPTER FIFTEEN
October 11, Tuesday
Emma

Emma opened the front door of the house, her arms full of library books. Her eyes flicked to Kyle's Range Rover in the driveway and her heart skipped. He was home early.

What should she say?

Yesterday's 'goodnight' was packed with tension – the good kind – and today bore nothing but raw anticipation.

She had escaped the house this morning without seeing Kyle, which was a small victory, given how early he normally woke up on Tuesdays.

But she had spent all day editing her latest steamy romance and she was primed to explode. She knew it was a good scene when she was able to turn herself on.

The October sun beat down, unseasonably warm, as she walked up the front steps of Kyle's house. When she quietly opened the front door, she hoped she'd be able to sneak around to her bedroom and not have to think of something brilliant and charming to say.

Except she couldn't be so lucky. When she saw him, she stopped dead.

Kyle stood at the grill on the patio, shirtless, flipping veggie burgers. His tanned, jacked back was to her, sculpted muscles shifting under tawny skin as he moved with an easy grace.

Emma froze, heat flooding her body. She traced the familiar lines of his broad shoulders, the dip of his spine, the cut of his hips rising from worn jeans. Her mouth went dry.

Man, he was gorgeous.

Memories flickered through her mind involuntarily – the feel of his hands on her body, his lips claiming hers, the solid warmth of him against and inside her.

Emma swallowed hard, cheeks flaming. She forced herself to look away from Kyle, taking a deep breath to clear her clouded mind.

Get a grip.

"Hey Em, veggie-burgers are almost ready," Kyle called, turning to face her with a grin. Apparently he knew she was standing there, staring. His deep brown eyes gleamed in the sun, crinkling at the corners.

Emma's gaze snagged onto the dark trail of hair below his navel before jerking back to his face. She clutched her books tighter, as if they could shield her pounding heart from view.

"Starving," she managed, summoning a smile.

Stay focused on the food. Do not think about running her hands over every inch of him, tasting the salt on his skin—

"Need any help?" Kyle asked, brows furrowing.

Emma shook her head, avoiding his eyes. "I'm fine. Be right back."

She hurried through the house on shaky legs, dropping the books on the entry table.

This was bad. Very bad.

How was she going to make it through the evening without combusting?

Last night had opened a whole new can of worms.

Didn't her life have enough worms?

Emma pressed a cool hand to her flaming cheek and took a deep breath.

She could do this. Just act normal.

Right. Normal. She squared her shoulders and walked back onto the deck, pulse racing. This was going to be the longest meal of her life.

Kyle eyed Emma curiously as she returned and took a seat at the patio table. "Everything okay?"

"Of course." Emma summoned a bright smile and folded her hands in her lap to hide their faint tremor. "Smells amazing."

"Hope you're hungry." Kyle set a plate in front of her, loaded with a veggie burger and fresh greens. "Made extra."

Emma's stomach growled, though she had little appetite for food. She took a bite and nearly moaned at the burst of flavor that hit her tongue.

Kyle's lips quirked up. "Good?"

She nodded, unable to speak. His gaze felt like a caress, setting her nerve endings aflame. Emma stared at her plate, acutely aware of Kyle in her periphery as he ate.

She could see the muscles in his arm flexing with each movement, could imagine how they would feel shifting under her palms—

"You're being awfully quiet." Kyle nudged her foot under the table with his, sending a jolt through her. "Everything going okay with your book?"

Emma's face heated as she thought of the steamy love scene she'd been editing. "It's, um. Going well."

"Yeah?" His voice was a low rumble, like distant thunder.

She risked a glance at him and immediately regretted it. He was watching her with a hooded, intense gaze that made her tongue dry up. Emma fumbled for a water glass and took a long drink, willing her raging pulse to slow.

"The, uh, tension between the characters is building," she said, avoiding his eyes.

"Is it, now?" Kyle's foot bumped into her calf as he shifted. Jury was out on whether it was on purpose. "What kind of tension?"

A shockwave of heat rolled through Emma's body. She was way in over her head, here.

She stood abruptly, nearly knocking over her chair. "I should get back to writing."

Kyle eyebrows drew together. "Em, did I do something—"

"No, no you're fine," Emma said hastily. She gathered the remains of her meal with trembling hands. "Just...inspired."

She risked a glance at Kyle's puzzled expression as she retreated to the sanctuary of her bedroom, pulse thundering. She leaned against the now-locked door, eyes closed, willing her body to calm. But it was no use. Every inch of her skin felt hypersensitive, attuned to the memory of Kyle's gaze, his touch. Her heart pounded as she drew in a deep, steadying breath.

She had to get a grip. This was her ex-husband, for God's sake, not some romance hero.

But her traitorous body refused to listen to reason. Heat pooled low in her belly at the thought of Kyle's potency, the raw masculinity he exuded without even trying. She swallowed hard, thighs clenching against the ache building inside her.

She couldn't stop picturing what it would feel like to have his hands on her body, instead of her own. To feel his lips and tongue teasing her most sensitive flesh...

What was she doing? This was madness. Pure, unadulterated madness.

Yet, she couldn't stop herself. Couldn't resist the siren call of forbidden pleasure, the temptation of Kyle's touch, even if only in her imagination.

Emma peeled her sundress over her head in a smooth motion and then tossed it aside. The brush of the fabric sliding over her sensitized skin made her shiver with delight.

She slowly undressed, savoring the building sense of arousal and impending release, and approached the bed.

She unhooked her bra and let it drop from her outstretched arm, then shimmied out of her panties, leaving them in a damp heap on the floor.

The air in the room felt cool against her overheated body, raising goosebumps along her flesh.

With a soft sigh, Emma sank onto the bed and stretched out on her back, limbs loose and pliant.

Anticipation hummed through her veins like an electric current as she gave herself over to the fantasy playing out in her mind. Her eyes slid closed as her fingers traced a path of longing across her skin, marking the paths she wanted Kyle's hands and mouth to take..

Emma's hands drifted over her body, fingertips skimming along her collarbone, between her breasts and down over her stomach. In the heat of her mind's eye, it was Kyle touching her: stroking her, igniting her passion with each feather-light caress.

She intentionally avoided the scar on her left breast.

A whimper caught in her throat as her thumbs teased her nipples into hard little peaks. Kyle's hands were much larger than her own. His grip would be firm and self-assured. Possessive. He would knead her flesh thoroughly, pinching and rolling her nipples until she was writhing beneath him.

She slid one hand lower, fingers dipping into her wet heat. Her back arched off the bed as she circled her clit, building the pressure with each pass.

In her mind, Kyle's lips were on her neck, teeth nipping at her pulse point before his tongue soothed the sting away. His hard body was molded into her softer curves, his erection a hot brand against her hip.

Emma's fingers moved faster, thrusting inside as the fantasy consumed her. She was so close, hovering on the edge of bliss. All she needed was one last little push to send her tumbling over...

She cried out as her orgasm crashed in ruthless waves, Kyle's name a mere exhale on her lips. Her inner walls clenched around her fingers as she rode out the intensity of her pleasure.

When her breathing finally slowed, Emma withdrew her hand and opened her eyes. The room was empty of the man she loved, the fantasy fading as reality crept back in.

Though sated for now, a hollow ache remained in the pit of her stomach. No matter how vivid her imagination, it was a poor substitute for the real thing. She wanted Kyle, not some conjured illusion. She wanted his hands on her body, his kiss on her lips as they came together.

Emma sighed, dragging a hand through her hair.

How much longer was she supposed to live with him? She couldn't run to her room every night whenever he did something sexy.

She'd be getting fifty thousand steps a day.

And he'd probably think she developed a severe case of IBS.

Was it possible to spontaneously combust from sheer lust?

She smiled at the thought, warmth flooding her cheeks. After so many years apart, it was almost embarrassing how much she still wanted him.

Emma rose from the bed on unstable legs and cleaned off before sliding back under the covers. It was still early, but there was no way she'd be able to look him in the eye for the rest of the night.

Sleeping naked in his house gave her such a taboo wiggle of pleasure down below that she left her PJs off and gloried in the feel of his silky sheets on her sensitive flesh.

And if she played with herself again a little while later...well, that was her business.

· · · • · • · • · · ·

Emma woke the next morning, still basking in the afterglow of her fantasy. She stretched with a contented sigh, the events of the previous night playing through her mind.

Though she knew she should get up and start her day, she couldn't quite bring herself to leave the cozy warmth of her bed just yet. Not when she could stay here dreaming of Kyle and all the ways she wanted him to make love to her.

A knock on her bedroom door startled her from her reverie. "Emma, are you up, yet?" Kyle's voice filtered through the wood, sending a thrill down her spine.

She sat up, clutching the sheet to her chest as her heart raced. What was he doing here? They usually kept to their separate spaces in the mornings until they were both ready to face the day.

"Just a minute," she called back, scrambling out of bed to find something to wear. She grabbed a silk robe from her closet and belted it around her waist, just as another knock sounded at the door.

"I'm coming in," Kyle warned, and the door creaked open.

Hadn't she locked that?

Emma's mouth went desert dry at the sight of him. Kyle stood in the doorway wearing only a pair of low-slung sweatpants, his hair mussed from sleep and his gaze heavy-lidded.

Yikes. He was gorgeous.

Her fingers itched to run through his hair and over the hard planes of his chest.

She swallowed hard, clutching her robe tighter. "What is it?"

A slow, devastating smile curved his lips. "I thought we could have breakfast together this morning. If you're interested, that is. I know you didn't eat much last night and we didn't get to see each other much yesterday. You were gone before I even got up for practice."

Emma's heart stuttered.

Oh, my.

Kyle's eyes glinted with amusement and something more – a hunger that had nothing to do with breakfast. Emma's pulse leapt as she met his gaze, anticipation coiling low in her belly.

"I—um, sure," she said after a pause, hating how breathless she sounded. "Just give me a few minutes to get ready."

Kyle's smile widened. "Take your time. I still need to get ready too. I'll meet you in the kitchen." He pulled the door closed behind him, leaving Emma staring after him in stunned silence.

She didn't miss the way his eyes had skimmed her scantily clad body before he left.

And that wasn't a cell phone in his pocket...

Her lips curled into a bemused smile as she turned toward her closet to get dressed.

Today was shaping up to be an interesting day indeed.

CHAPTER SIXTEEN

October 12, Wednesday
Kyle

The cool night air brushed against Kyle's skin as they strolled down the dimly lit sidewalk, their shoulders bumping and hands grazing with each step. It was getting darker earlier and earlier; this time, a month ago, it would have been as bright as day.

"You're getting slow in your old age," Emma teased. "I can't believe I beat you up that hill."

Kyle snorted. "You got lucky. My knee has been acting up, again, and it was a tough practice today."

"Excuses, excuses." Her eyes glinted with mirth under the low glow of the streetlights.

He nudged her with his elbow. "Keep talking and I'll make you run extra laps at the gym when I sneak in with you tomorrow."

"You wouldn't dare!"

His lips quirked. "Try me."

Emma bumped him back, the scent of her shampoo wafting over him, and his stomach did a slow roll. Tonight felt different. Charged. Every point of contact between them sent sparks dancing across his skin.

He cleared his throat and gazed forward.

His ex-wife. Off limits.

Good friend material, maybe.

Not good...whatever-they-were-dancing-around material.

However, when she laughed, bright and carefree, and slipped her arm through his, heat flooded his veins.

He was in trouble here, and he knew it.

They arrived at the house a few minutes later and Kyle unlocked the door, then disarmed the alarm.

They made their way into the kitchen, a happy silence between them. He felt her turn down the hallway and he let out a sigh.

Maybe now he'd get a chance to route the blood flow back to some more vital organs rather than the one that was currently hijacking the supply.

Kyle bent down and rummaged through the fridge. His gaze snagged on a pack of organic beer, and he snorted. Once upon a time, Emma could outdrink him without trying. Now she fretted over preservatives and "toxic" ingredients.

He shook his head, grabbing a bottle of the wacky beer. He tried a swig, ignoring the bitter, vegetal taste. As much as he missed her old curves, he couldn't deny the new Emma was sexy as hell – so maybe she was onto something with all this organic shit.

"So much for all those organic antioxidants, huh?"

Kyle jumped, sloshing beer over his hands. Emma came up next to him and grabbed her own beer and she crossed her arms with a knowing look.

"You're still here."

She cocked her head and looked at him funny. "Yeah, where else would I be?"

"I thought you went to your bedroom."

"And so you decided to steal my beer while I wasn't looking?"

Heat flooded his cheeks, and he swore under his breath.

Smooth, Justice. Real smooth.

Her head cocked to the side and she watched him curiously.

Because he was acting like an idiot.

An organic beer stealing idiot.

"You never told me what your contact at the station said today when you called him." She took a dainty sip and leaned against the counter next to him, looking up into his face, her eyes searching his.

What was she looking for?

"They have nothing new to report," Kyle said, dumping the beer down the sink and pouring himself a glass of water. "Just a dead end on that security footage. The guy is a ghost."

Emma's fingers tightened around the cool glass. "I don't understand how he could just vanish into thin air like that. He had to come from somewhere."

"He's careful. Meticulous." Anger simmered in Kyle's gut, hot and acrid. If he ever got his hands on the bastard, he'd—

"Kyle." Emma's gentle tone pulled him from his darkening thoughts. "I know you're worried but try not to do anything rash. Let the police handle this."

"And if they can't?" He slammed a fist on the counter, the glass in his hand shuddering. "What if something happens to you while they have their thumbs up their asses?"

Emma pushed away from the counter and laid a hand on his forearm. "Nothing is going to happen. We're taking precautions, the police are on alert. I'll be fine."

He searched her face, looking for any trace of fear or doubt, but found only calm determination. Even after everything, Emma remained strong. It was one of the many things he loved about her.

As they stood in the dimly lit kitchen, Kyle felt the familiar tug of concern for Emma, his instinct to protect her coming on as strong as ever. Her words were soothing, but he couldn't shake the nagging worry that clung to his mind like a persistent shadow.

He leaned against the countertop, his eyes never leaving her face. "I just can't shake this feeling of being powerless, Em. Like I'm failing you by not doing more."

Emma's gaze softened, her fingers tracing soothing circles on his arm. "You're not failing me, Kyle. Remember? I promised I'd be honest. And you're not failing me. We're all just...doing the best we can."

Why did she look so guilty?

His phone buzzed with a reminder, jolting him from his thoughts. He cursed under his breath, as he checked it, realizing he had completely forgotten about the reservation at Versailles. It was an elite restaurant on a rooftop terrace in the heart of the city. It was hell to get reservations.

"Damn, I can't believe I spaced on this." He showed her the notification on his phone. "I made this dinner reservation with Jaz months ago, but I completely forgot to cancel it after we broke up."

Emma's surprise was evident. "Woah. Versailles? You don't mess around with flames, huh? Nothing but the best?"

Was she...jealous?

Kyle filed that away for later and then explained, to calm the awakening dragon. "It's just a nice place to eat, there was no special occasion."

She pinched her lips together and then closed her eyes. Emma shook her head and then opened her eyes, her face now twisted in embarrassment. "Sorry. I shouldn't care. Just caught me off guard. She had good taste. I love her chair on the patio." Emma paused to look outside and then looked back at him. "I'm assuming that was hers?"

Kyle nodded and narrowed his eyes on her.

Was he in trouble?

He felt like he was in trouble...

They exchanged a look, the tension fading as they both realized how absurd the situation was. A wry smile tugged at the corners of Emma's lips. "Well, I guess it would be a shame to waste a reservation. What do you say we go to Versailles?"

Relief washed over Kyle, and he couldn't hide his grin. "I'm game."

She headed into her room to shower and dress up and he did the same.

When he got into the shower and started washing off, he was struck with the thought that Emma was in her own shower doing the exact same thing.

Once he opened that Pandora's box, the fantasies took hold and didn't let go. As the hot water cascaded over him, he allowed his mind to wander.

He imagined Emma's body pressed against his, the steam and water enveloping them. Their hands exploring each other's curves, lips crashing together in a passionate embrace.

As he closed his eyes, the memory of her laughter and the way her eyes sparkled when she teased him flooded his mind. He could almost feel the warmth of her presence, as if she were right there with him in the steamy enclosure.

His breathing quickened as he lost himself in the vivid images, the thrill of the fantasy consuming him. His hand moved of its own accord, igniting sensations that left him breathless and wanting.

A surge of pleasure coursed through him, and he groaned out his release. He leaned heavily against the cool tile wall, his heart pounding.

His steamy reverie was shattered when, amidst his heavy breaths, he heard Emma scream.

Panic surged through him and he charged from his shower.

Emma's wail had been laced with enough fear that there was no time to process turning off the water or grabbing a towel.

He burst into her room to find her standing, wrapped in a towel, her eyes wide with terror as she pointed to her dresser.

In it was a sight that chilled him to the core – a writhing mass of venomous snakes were slithering around in the open drawer.

Kyle pulled her close, and steered them from the scene, his eyes resting on every possible hiding spot as he dragged her into his room and locked the door.

They needed to get out of there. Immediately.

Clearly, his alarm system was fucked.

After carefully opening his own drawers to pull out clothes, he quickly checked them before pulling them on. He grabbed a couple extras and found a bag in the corner. Emma was still frozen by the door. He tossed the duffel on his shoulder and entered the hall, again checking for signs of an intruder. He pulled Emma into her room and again locked the door as he found random clothes for her in her dresser and closet. He threw them in the bag with his things and went to her again.

"My phone's in the kitchen."

"Same."

He gave her a somber nod. "You with me? You okay?"

Her blue eyes looked into his and his heart squeezed.

There it was.

The hurt, a mile deep, that Ryan told him about.

Fuck.

Forget a mile deep. It was ten.

His heart twisted.

He refocused himself, and after taking some deep breaths, brought them back into the hall, to the alarm panel, where a click of a red button triggered it, and out of the house.

Checking the back seat of his car to make sure no one was waiting, time pushed on him.

Every second she was here was a risk to her.

Emma needed to be safe.

Now.

His hands shaking from adrenaline, he loaded her up, and peeled out of the driveway.

When he was on the road and the house was in his rearview, he called the police.

He'd give them one more day. If they couldn't find the fucker...then he was calling Mickey's guy.

Because there was no fucking way he was going to let any psycho touch a fucking hair on Emma's head.

CHAPTER SEVENTEEN

October 12, Wednesday
Kyle

After a series of quick phone calls, Kyle drove them to a house out in Southwick. Apparently it was a short-term rental, so it had everything they'd need except groceries. With a laser-like focus, Kyle guided them through a local grocery store, his eyes darting across the shelves as he efficiently loaded a small basket of essentials.

And that was that.

After dinner at their hideaway, Emma and Kyle worked to clean up the tiny kitchen. Emma wiped the counters with a damp cloth while Kyle washed the dishes and placed them methodically in the drying rack. Each of their movements were so precise that it felt like their limbs would snap off if they bumped into anything.

"Remember when you used to make fun of me for being so organized?" Emma asked, the tension finally getting her to break the silence.

Kyle cracked a small smile. "I apologize for my past self. I've learned the error in my ways."

"Apology accepted."

Silence fell.

"Your turn to pick the movie," Kyle reminded her, wiping his hands dry on a tea towel.

"Right," she walked over to the TV and scrolled through the options. "Prepare yourself for an amazing rom com, my friend."

"Can't wait," he deadpanned.

As Emma searched for the perfect movie, Kyle went about double-checking all the locks on the doors and windows, ensuring the curtains were drawn tight. He also reviewed the rental's security system.

"All right, I think I found the one," Emma announced, settling on the couch and curling her legs beneath her.

"Let's see it, then," Kyle replied, joining her and throwing an arm along the back of the couch.

He was touching her.

Again.

She glanced at Kyle and found his gaze already on her, his deep eyes filled with a mix of longing and uncertainty.

"Are you sure about this movie?" he asked.

"Absolutely," she replied, her own voice wavering ever so slightly. "I've heard good things about it."

"Alrighty then," he agreed, shifting his focus back to the screen.

But Emma knew that neither of them were really paying attention to the love story unfolding before their eyes when they were both too focused by the one they were dancing around. Their thoughts were consumed by the past, the emotions they still harbored for one another, and the unknown future that lay ahead.

"Are you even watching this?" Kyle teased, catching her looking his way again.

"Of course," Emma replied, feigning innocence, "I just can't help but admire how good you look tonight."

"Nice try," he gave a barely there smile that had her heart racing. "But we do need to talk about what happened tonight. Are you okay?"

"Nope, I'm fine," she deflected, turning her gaze back to the screen.

If she could never see a snake again...that'd be cool.

But the image of him bursting into her room like a naked Clark Kent was something that might be worth revisiting nightly.

Lordy, he was built.

And hung like a freaking moose.

"Remember how often we used to quote movies and TV shows to each other?" Emma asked, her voice soft and nostalgic.

"Like *Friends*?" Kyle responded, a small smile playing on his lips.

"Exactly," Emma laughed, a warmth spreading through her chest as she reminisced on their shared love of film.

"Those were good times," Kyle admitted, his eyes meeting hers briefly before returning to the screen.

Emma couldn't resist pushing further, allowing herself to indulge in the charged energy between them, embracing the way the arousal made her feel. Anything was better than focusing on the terror that was waiting on standby. "Remember those late-night make-out sessions on the couch?"

Kyle coughed, "How could I forget? Pretty sure one of those gave us our first pregnancy scare," he said, shaking his head.

"Birth control is a wonderful thing. I miss those days." She gave a wistful sigh and then offered up a wry smile. "Not the pregnancy scares. But the...connection. The friendship we had. Not a day goes by that I don't grieve for what we lost."

There. A confession.

Honesty.

"Who says they're gone for good?" Kyle shot back, his voice low.

Emma's breath hitched, her body responding to his words as if they were a physical touch. She swallowed, trying to maintain her composure. "Well, I guess there's that."

"Guess so," he murmured.

Even so, neither of them made a move.

Emma shifted in her seat, uncomfortable with all the tension. The movement caused a spot in her back to crack into the silence and she winced. Emma stretched her neck, wincing slightly as it shot down her back. "I missed my weekly appointment with Jen," she explained. "My body's used to the deluxe treatment nowadays. Plus, with how fast the words were coming, I felt like I had to get them out of me as quickly as possible."

"Maybe you should try dictating instead?" Kyle watched her closely, waiting for something...

"Dictation helps during the drafting phase, but for me, it always ends up with more edits later," Emma sighed, trying to ignore the way Kyle's gaze lingered on her. "My body appreciates it more during the dictation time, though."

Kyle's eyes were conflicted, a battle of longing and uncertainty raged, "Well, I could give you a neck rub during the movie if you want? But don't think I don't know what you're doing, you minx." He ended on a tease and Emma's heart did a little dance in her chest.

A neck rub?

Yes, please.

A neck rub from Kyle...

Different kettle of fish.

Back in the day, a back rub was never just a back rub for them.

However, the temptation of having his strong hands work on her aching neck proved too powerful.

"All right," she agreed.

Man, she hoped she wouldn't regret this later.

Emma hesitated for a moment, her heart pounding in her chest, before she finally sat down on the couch in front of Kyle as the movie played on in the background. She tried to ignore the butterflies fluttering in her stomach as he attempted to massage her neck and shoulders over her thick tee shirt. The fabric bunched up, causing a rough scraping of the fabric against her skin and preventing him from applying enough pressure to work out the knots.

"Emma," he said with a chuckle, "I sound like a cheap rom com pick up line, but this isn't going to work with your shirt on. You need to take it off."

Her cheeks flushed with embarrassment.

He was right, but still.

Oh boy.

With a deep breath, she reached down and pulled her tee shirt over her head, doing her best to remain modest by keeping her back facing him.

"Better?" she asked, trying to keep her voice steady.

"Better," he grunted back.

As Kyle began to massage her neck and shoulders again, Emma felt too exposed in just her sports bra. His fingers grazed against the thin fabric, making her shiver with a mixture of arousal and anxiety.

His fingers tried to roll down her neck but kept getting interrupted on their long and leisurely path by her sports bra.

"Uh, Em," he said, sounding almost apologetic. " I keep hitting your bra. Can you slide the straps down somehow? Or...something? I need to step out and get some lotion or oil anyway, so you can have some privacy."

He traveled with oil?

Kyle chuckled, reading her mind. "It's in my travel bag. Professional athlete, remember? Jen makes us all our own mixes so we can do our own self-massages if things get too painful before we can get in to see her."

Oh.

Jen always was a smart cookie.

Still, Emma hesitated, a whirlwind of emotions swirling within her – nervousness, excitement, reluctance, and the undeniable spark of arousal. As terrible of an idea this was...she gave a small nod to the TV, refusing to look back at him.

Once alone, Emma took several deep breaths to steady herself. There was no way she was removing it, not with the evidence of her treatment all those years before. Instead, she pulled her arms out of the straps and tucked them in, so it was like a micro tube top..

While she waited for Kyle, Emma tried to keep the nervous energy at bay. She knew the boundaries they were pushing but couldn't deny the desire that coursed through her veins.

With each touch, each lingering glance, they were teetering on the edge of something powerful and all-consuming – a force that threatened to engulf them both if they let it.

"All right, I'm back," Kyle announced as he returned to the living room, his voice tinged with a playful edge. He sat down behind Emma on the couch, squirting some massage oil onto his hands. The scent of vanilla filled the air, calming Emma's nerves slightly.

Vanilla and sandalwood. Intoxicating. Who knew?

"Can you put your hair up higher?" He asked. "I don't want to make a mess."

The dirty part of her mind purred at that. She slapped the naughty vixen away.

"Sure," Emma replied, clumsily twisting her long hair into a higher bun. Despite her best efforts, a few wispy strands escaped and fell. She was so hyper focused on Kyle behind her, she just embraced the fact that the strands were going to get oily.

A combination of nerves and the chilly room had her shivering slightly as she held her shirt against her chest.

Modesty, warmth, or protection?

Maybe all three.

Kyle positioned himself behind her, his large hands hovering above her shoulders for a moment before finally making contact. "Ready?"

Emma took a deep breath before leaning back into his strong, muscular frame.

"Is this okay?" He asked, his voice was rough.

"Y-Yeah," Emma stammered, struggling to maintain her composure as Kyle's fingers dug into her tight muscles. His rough, calloused hands began working on her tense muscles, rubbing the fragrant oil into her skin.

She couldn't help but feel a surge of desire course through her at his touch, but she stubbornly clung to the idea that this was nothing more than a friendly gesture.

"Your neck *is* really tight," Kyle observed, his fingers kneading the stubborn knots.

Good. Conversation would distract them from the intimacy of their situation.

"Told you."

"You really shouldn't have skipped your visit with Jen."

"Yeah," she agreed, rolling her head back and letting her eyes drift shut as his hands worked their magic. "But crap was swirling, and the timing just wasn't right this week."

She let out a small moan of appreciation, and she could feel him tense behind her.

"Sorry," she murmured, embarrassed by her involuntary reaction.

"Don't apologize," he replied, his voice low and husky. "I'm glad I can help you feel better."

As Kyle continued to massage her neck, Emma found it increasingly difficult to focus on anything but the feel of his hands against her skin.

Talk about playing with fire.

Uncharacteristically the rebel, she allowed herself to sink deeper into the sensation, her body betraying her resolve as she leaned into his touch.

"Did anyone ever tell you that you have the most stubborn knots?" Kyle teased, pressing his thumbs into a particularly tight spot above her shoulder blade. Emma winced and then laughed in response.

"Jen would never insult her most prestigious client," she retorted, trying to keep her tone light despite the heat rising within her.

This was a mistake. She still didn't have her answer from the hospital.

Not to mention there was a person that was tormenting her.

This had a high likelihood of ending in disaster.

Another heartbreak.

Yet...

Maybe this could be their closure. Their goodbye.

She promised him she'd be honest, and she would be, but for right now, maybe she'd just...give herself this tiny taste of freedom. This tiny piece of heaven.

And if it helped them part ways as fond friends, then maybe it was all worth it.

Sure, he'd mourn her if her cancer won. But he'd have happy memories with her to drown out the last decade of growing resentment.

A peace filled her.

It wasn't a perfect situation.

But it was what she had to work with and she was so sick of trying to push him away.

"Thanks for this, Ky," she said, a small smile playing on her lips.

Kyle's hands paused for a moment before continuing their mission. "Feeling better?"

"Much."

Their eyes met briefly in the reflection of the TV screen and her breath caught.

"Good," Kyle murmured, his hands resuming their magical dance on Emma's skin.

Apparently, they were continuing the dangerous game they were playing.

The movie played on, but neither of them paid it any attention.

"Damn, your muscles are really knotted up," Kyle commented, his breath hot against Emma's ear.

She shivered involuntarily at the sensation, trying to keep herself in check despite her growing arousal.

"Occupational hazard," Emma quipped, attempting to maintain some semblance of normalcy even as Kyle's skilled hands continued to stoke the fire within her. "You should see what writing does to my wrists."

"Maybe I'll give them some attention later," he teased, his fingertips brushing ever so lightly over the curve of her collarbone.

"Promises, promises," she retorted, swallowing hard as an involuntary gasp escaped her lips when Kyle hit a particularly sensitive spot.

"Is that a challenge?" Kyle murmured, his voice low and seductive. Somehow, the simple question seemed weighted with so much more meaning than either of them was willing to address directly.

"Wouldn't dream of it," Emma replied, unable to keep the tremor from her voice.

Danger, danger.

Kyle's hands moved gently down her arms, pausing briefly to knead her tense forearms before making his way back up to her shoulders. As his fingers brushed against her neck, Emma felt a shiver run down her spine.

"Emma," Kyle whispered, his hand reaching forward and around to gently brush against her cheek. She turned her head slightly, eyes zeroing in on his intense expression.

It was now or never – a choice between giving in to their simmering desires or pulling back from the precipice.

"Kyle," she breathed, her voice barely audible above the sound of their ragged breaths.

And with that single word, the die was cast.

The flickering light from the TV screen cast an ethereal glow on Kyle's face as Emma tried to steady her breathing.

Kyle leaned in, pausing for a moment as if awaiting permission before placing a tender kiss on the nape of her neck. The sudden intimacy of his touch sent a jolt through her body and she couldn't help but release a soft gasp.

"Kyle..." she whispered, turning around to face him. Her arms instinctively held her shirt to her chest, unwilling to broach that subject yet.

Honesty was one thing, airing all the dirty laundry was another.

He met her gaze, and she saw the desire burning behind his eyes – a mirror to her own. Without another word, Emma closed the distance and their lips crashed together in a passionate and long-awaited kiss.

Chapter Eighteen

October 12, Wednesday
Emma

"Fuck, I've missed this," Kyle murmured against her lips, his hands finding purchase on her waist. His touch was both familiar and new.

Exhilarating.

"Me too." She allowed herself to be pulled closer to him. Their bodies moved in sync, guided by muscle memory and the shared history that bound them together.

As they lost themselves in each other's embrace, the room seemed to come alive with a mix of desire and tenderness, each touch a dance of rediscovery and vulnerability. The rom com playing on the TV screen was all but forgotten, replaced by the symphony of their mingled breaths and heartbeats.

"Emma," Kyle whispered between kisses, his voice rough with emotion. "I never...I never stopped loving you."

Her chest squeezed tight and her heart ached.

Oh, how she wished things had been different.

Why did cancer have to choose her?

Emma pulled back just enough to meet his eyes. "I was right there with you, honey." The words hung heavy in the air.

"Then, why?" His voice was tight. Desperate. Pained. "Why did you break us?"

Emma closed her eyes tight and rested her forehead against his, panting while she tried to regain some control. "Ky..."

What was she supposed to say?

"If I promise I'll tell you in the next few weeks, will that be okay?"

She was finally scheduled for a scan on Friday, so realistically she'd probably have a result within the next few days. In the off chance they postponed or needed a follow-up scan, she built in a time buffer to not only get her answer, and to drum up the courage to confess as well.

Kyle leaned his forehead harder into hers and his eyes watched her. The pain and confusion there on his face was killing her but she wasn't ready. Her trauma, her PTSD, her wounds...she just couldn't go there with him yet.

Not without risking his wrath for her choice.

And she knew it would be a rage unlike the world had ever seen.

Her Kyle. There's no way he wouldn't react poorly to the news that she left him when she found out she had cancer so he could go on living his dream while she battled for her life.

There was no way he'd take that peacefully.

As he probably shouldn't.

But what was done...was done.

And they were moving on.

Maybe...together?

"Where do we go from here?" He asked, his dark eyes searching hers for an answer she wasn't sure she had.

"One step at a time," she suggested, her fingers tracing the curve of his jaw. "Tackle today."

He gave her the world's most heart-wrenching, soul-shattering, stomach-clenching, toe-curling smile.

Wow.

"Tackle today," he agreed, leaning in to capture her lips once more. "Honesty, and in a few weeks, transparency. That's all I want, Ems," he murmured against her skin, his calloused hands tracing a path along her sides that left goosebumps in their wake. "We're finally exactly where we're meant to be."

Emma couldn't help but shiver at his words, her voice breathless. "Honesty and transparency, honey. I promise."

He peppered her collarbone with light kisses, causing her to bend her neck to give him better access. Emma reveled in the sensation of his strong arms holding her close, the heat of his body a welcome contrast to the rapidly cooling air of the room. Absently, she registered that Kyle's phone was vibrating on the side coffee table, but a wandering hand brought her attention back to Kyle and their reunion.

As the intensity of their connection built, their movements grew more urgent and desperate. Hands roamed hungrily over familiar yet long-forgotten terrain, rediscovering the valleys and peaks of one another's bodies. Each touch was a revelation, a reminder of all they had once shared and all that still lay before them.

"God, Ems," Kyle whispered, his voice strained as he pressed his lips to her temple. "I've missed you so damn much."

"Me too," Emma admitted, her heart aching with the truth of her words. It was as if a piece of her soul had been missing all these years, only to finally reappear.

"Are you ready to do this?" He asked, his eyes dark with desire as he gazed down at her. "For me, it feels like we're just picking up where we left off, but I don't know where you're at with this."

Kyle. Her sweet, protective Kyle.

She raised a hand to his face and splayed her palm and fingers over the black bristles there. "Kyle..."

This was it. There was no going back if she did this...

"Hey," he said softly, sensing her hesitation. "We don't have to do anything you're not ready for, Em. We can take things slow, all right?"

"That's not it," she whispered. "We never ended for me either. I just...come with baggage now. And I just don't want to drag you down with me when life gets...*messy.*"

"I don't know if you remember this or not, Emma Justice, but I know how to use a laundry machine now and know my way around a dishwasher. Hell, I've cleaned my bathroom a time or two since we split. I know how to handle '*messy.*' Like we established earlier: four hands are better than one."

Her sweet, sweet Kyle. She didn't even bother correcting the incorrect last name.

She dove back into him, kissing him hard. He might not deserve what's coming to him, but if he wanted honesty, he'd get it. He'd get all of her. Then, he could be the one to decide what to keep.

Their bodies moved together with renewed fervor. Clothing was torn from bodies and their hands and lips were everywhere. Every inch of skin was free for the taking. When Kyle tried to slide her out of her bra, she stopped him.

"I want it on."

He gave her a confused look before continuing his exploration. With how detailed his hands and mouth were going, one would think he majored in cartography. There wasn't an inch of her that he wasn't re-imprinting in his memory. Every new freckle, scar, curve, or dimple was his to explore, taste and touch.

He re-learned her body with a devouring hunger that threatened to consume her. All that she could do was writhe and try to fight him for her own chance at exploring him.

Eventually, he let her, but only after he gave her a mind-numbing orgasm with his mouth.

Eagerly, she retried to return the favor.

It had been so long...

"Em...time for a position change." Kyle gasped out, his voice strained with effort.

Immediately, she released him and pushed up off the floor from between his legs. She climbed onto his lap and placed a wet kiss on his lips.

She gave him a heavy look, waiting for his nod, before lowering herself onto him.

Heaven.

Emma threw her head back and gloried in the length of him in her. Filling her.

Completing her.

But not for long.

Kyle grabbed her cheek and pulled her face back down to his for a ravenous kiss, meanwhile thrusting up and into her.

Emma's heart raced as she clung to him, her nails digging into the hard muscles of his back. Their breaths mingled, heavy and ragged, as they moved together in a primal dance of passion and desire. The room was filled with the sounds of their union, echoing off the walls and filling the space with an electric energy that seemed to crackle in the air.

"Work with me, Em. How close are you, baby?" Kyle ground out; his voice strained with effort.

Emma was beyond caring about restraint or propriety; all she wanted was to feel that rush of ecstasy with Kyle. The love of her life. Her person. Her reason.

"Please," she whispered, her voice barely audible over the pounding of their bodies. "Almost there. I just need...I need this...I need you."

At her words, something seemed to snap inside of him, and he turned up his efforts. Then they were both hurtling toward that sweet release they so desperately craved.

As the waves of pleasure crashed over them, Emma let out a cry of pure, unbridled joy – the sound as raw and powerful as the emotions that tore through her very soul.

"Fuck, Emma..." Kyle breathed, his voice shaking as he collapsed back into the couch, pulling her close to his chest. Their sweat-slicked bodies trembled from the intensity of their shared climax.

For several long moments, they simply lay there, trying to catch their breath and come back down to Earth.

As their breathing slowly returned to normal, Emma noticed the uncertainty that flickered across Kyle's face. "Kyle?" she ventured hesitantly, her fingers tracing idle patterns on his damp skin as she waited for him to respond.

"Yeah?"

"I love you," she whispered, her eyes filling with tears as she clung to him even tighter. "No matter what happened back then. No matter what happens next. I'll always love you."

He gave her a small smile, using a free finger to twirl some hair that had fallen out of her bun.

"I hated this, you know. Couldn't figure out why you'd go and change your hair when it was perfect the way it was." He paused his twirling and brought his eyes back to hers. "It's still perfect. Just different. Just like you're still that same quiet girl who sat next to me in eighth-grade math. You always had your nose in a book, and it *wasn't* an algebra book. And you had no idea how football was even played, but after coming to *one* game, you were *convinced* that I was going pro." His smile turned wistful as he looked up toward the ceiling. "You weren't even watching *me* that game. I was number twenty-three. You were watching thirty-two the whole game." He laughed at the memory and squeezed her tight, brushing his lips across her forehead. "I'll never forget how excited you were to see me that Monday and tell me all about how awesome my plays were. And here you were, talking about a completely different player."

"Kyle...you were thirty-two. I have a picture of us with you wearing—"

He looked down at her. "That afternoon I asked Coach if we could trade jerseys. Said my future wife was dyslexic with numbers and got me mixed up and I didn't want to break your heart." His smile turned sweet, or sweeter if that was possible. "I still can't believe he let me trade our jerseys." Kyle shook his head. "I can only imagine what was going through his head."

"I never knew..."

He leaned down and placed a soft kiss on her lips. "Of course not. It would have only made you sad. But...honesty. And plus, you're going to hear it all on Friday night during the Galloway Charitable Awards Night."

What?

Emma just blinked at him.

Kyle stole another kiss. "You'll be my date, right? My wife, ex-wife, whatever, should be my date. I shouldn't go stag to an awards ceremony where I'm actually receiving the award of the night..."

Emma jerked and sat upright, pushing away from his chest and ignoring the wet feeling where they were joined.

"What!"

He grinned. "Oh, did I forget to ment—"

She slapped at his pecs. "Kyle! You were awarded the Galloway Service Award this year?"

William, the team's owner, who was also Lexie's dad, only gave those out sporadically. They had a big party every year to give out other awards, but only when it was truly earned did he present someone with the Galloway Service Award. It only went to players on the team that he felt went above and beyond in their communities. It was a big deal.

Huge.

Kyle pulled her back in, also ignoring the growing wet patch that was no doubt starting to ruin the rented couch.

"Yeah, I got it. So, I have to give a speech. I figured that was a perfect way to start. Because without you, I never would have believed I could have made it. I probably would have failed out of my classes in college when we were there, and I never would have bothered to enter the draft. You made it all possible. Every step of the way. And I thank you for that. Hell, all the organizations that I've been able to help, should thank you for that."

Well...shit.

If he only knew the unknowing price he paid for that...

Honesty. She promised honesty.

Fine. Here goes.

As Emma opened her mouth to admit the price of his success, Kyle's phone started vibrating, again. Kyle wouldn't let her dismount long enough for him to answer it. Instead, he scooted over, grabbed it and looked at the screen.

He raised his eyebrows at her and turned the screen her way.

It was the investigator on her case.

At 10:00 pm on a Wednesday night.

This was either very good...or very bad.

CHAPTER NINETEEN

October 14, Friday
Kyle

The next morning, they went down to the station and stared at a lunatic in handcuffs, sitting behind a one-way mirror.

Duncan O'Brien, a name that meant nothing to them until now, sat disheveled and glassy-eyed. He looked every bit the part of a criminal and there was something about his wild gaze that sent shivers down Kyle's spine.

"I don't recognize him at all," Emma muttered, her fingers tightly interlocked at her belly as she leaned forward, squinting at the man through the glass. Her soft blue eyes darted around his features, searching for any hint of familiarity.

Kyle shook his head, exchanging a puzzled glance with the waiting officer. "I have no idea who he is, either."

"Well, he certainly knows one or both of you. The warrant to bring him in happened so fast that we were able to storm in and grab him when he wasn't ready. It helps your case that he has a sick, friggin' shrine of you two in his basement. Pictures, items, newspaper clippings, copies of your books. You name it. We got 'im. The guy is done."

"But how did he get the code to Kyle's house?" Emma's voice quivered with a mix of fear and confusion.

The officer shrugged. "We haven't got that far yet, and his lawyer stepped out for a bit. Plus, with him being so doped up...there's only so much we can do until he sobers up."

Apparently, he'd been high as a kite when they took him in. Judging by the track marks in his arm, it wasn't his first time chasing the dragon.

Emma moved closer to the glass, her breath fogging it as she strained to see any clues about the man. She glanced over her shoulder at Kyle. "Why does he hate me so much?"

Kyle reached out and gently squeezed her shoulder. "Don't know, Em. Some people are just deranged. Hopefully, they get some answers for us, but we might never really know."

Legally. They might not ever *legally* know. Because with or without the help of the cops, Kyle was sure as fuck going to get answers.

The cops had finally found a local doorbell camera that showed their shrouded mystery figure parking and walking to Emma's house. The same hooded figure that walked right up and into Kyle's. Using a series of random street cams and home security cameras, the cops were able to piece together the plate number and the car. A quick run through of their database and boom: Duncan O'Brien. It still didn't explain his infatuation with Emma though...

Emma leaned into him, her chest rising and falling rapidly as she continued to stare at the man who had made her life a living hell.

· · · · · · · · · · ·

Kyle's fingers fumbled with the knot of his tie, cursing under his breath as he struggled to tame the silk torture device. If they were at his house, he could just grab an easier tie, but nope, they were getting ready at Emma's, so she only had a small army's supply of makeup and...whatever else she needed for the awards banquet.

His mind raced with thoughts of last night, the memory of Emma in his arms, her lips against his – a sweet taste of redemption and desire – and he couldn't stop his smile.

This was their second chance, and they weren't going to mess it up this time. He could tell by the way she touched his cheek and stared at him when he wasn't looking.

She was *all* in.

So was he.

His publicist's voice droned on via his phone in the background, but all Kyle could see was Emma's smile; that damn irresistible smile that made his pulse flutter and his stomach tie into knots.

He needed to get it together. No one liked a man who was starry-eyed and showed it.

He paused his useless movements.

Well...the girls from the book club certainly seemed to like it when their men showed how besotted they were.

Hmm.

Not willing to fight with it anymore, he left the tie draped around his neck, stepped out of the guest room, and strode down the hall.

As he approached the door to Emma's bedroom, his steps faltered. She stood there, framed by the doorway like a vision from a dream. Her eyes caught his in the standing mirror's reflection, the blue depths shimmering like the sky. She was breathtaking, wearing a navy dress that hugged her thin frame in all the right places, reminding him that she was very much real.

Kyle's gaze lingered on her strawberry blonde hair cascading down her back like a waterfall. Fuck, she was perfect.

"You look amazing," he said, his voice surprisingly soft. He watched as a gentle blush bloomed on her cheeks, transforming her from stunning to downright irresistible.

Damn, he had missed this woman – her vulnerability, her strength, and her ability to turn him inside out with just a single glance.

"Thank you," Emma murmured, her eyes not leaving the reflection of his in the mirror. She finally turned to face him, her gaze locked onto his with a gravity that sent his pulse racing. "You clean up pretty well yourself, Mr. Fullback."

He chuckled, running a hand through his hair. "Only when I have somewhere important to be."

His heart rate picked up. She was here. This was real. She was really home.

It all came crashing into him and he felt the overwhelming need to...cry.

"Kyle?" Her voice lilted, pulling him out of his reverie. "What's up?"

He coughed into his fist and scratched at his cheek. "Nothing. Just admiring your dress."

"Mhm." Emma shot him a confused grin.

"Bet it looks better on the floor," he shot back.

"Ah." She rolled her eyes and stepped toward him. "And you need help with your tie. I see now." Her hands went to his chest, and he caught the softness of her signature rose perfume. Heaven's gardens couldn't possibly smell this good. "You can iron your clothes but can't tie a tie? Still?"

"I have people for that," he muttered, staring down at her, hypnotized.

Dates, he had *dates* that handled that for him. A decade worth of poor substitutes for the delicate fingers that were now adjusting the knot. Her touch was so light it made him shiver.

He was never going to learn to tie one, not if the alternative was her soft hands on him, taking care of him, and her smile on his face.

"Better?" she asked, stepping back to inspect her handiwork.

"Perfect," he replied, his voice rougher than he intended.

She was. She was everything. And finally, *right* where she belonged.

"Good luck, tonight," she said softly, her eyes conveying a mixture of love and happiness that tugged at his already fragile self-control.

His heart hammered in his chest as he reached out, gently cupping her cheek with his hand. The warmth of her skin seeped into his palm, igniting a fire that spread through his entire being. He leaned in, their lips mere inches apart, the air between them crackling with anticipation.

"I don't need luck. I have you."

She pinched her lips and looked toward her phone on the side table, her expression worried. Tingles went up his spine.

"Kyle," she said, her voice filled with vulnerability, "no matter what happens, I want you to know that I'm grateful for this second chance."

Kyle cocked his head and stared at her, trying to figure out what the hell she was worried about.

"Em, baby, we got the guy. We'll get our answers. Just let the cops and lawyers do their thing. And if we need more resources, we'll get more resources. Nothing bad is going to happen, baby. We're all set. We're golden. For the first time in a decade, we're together again, and we can breathe easy. Smooth sailing from here on out, honey."

Her eyes welled with tears and she pitched forward, resting her forehead into his throat.

"I promised you honesty. We need to talk about what happened. But tonight's not the time. Maybe after? We really just need to talk."

He dipped down and used a forefinger to bring up her chin.

"Baby, you're forgiven. Whatever your reasons, we're good now. We're moving on. Just breathe easy with me, okay?"

Emma bit her lip so hard that some of the damn red lipstick came off onto one of her white front teeth.

He gave her a soft smile and reached around her to grab a tissue. He nodded down at her mouth, and she took it, with a watery and conflicted smile. Slowly, not breaking eye contact, she wiped at her mouth and dabbed at her teeth. She had clearly done this before.

"Emma, we're going to make this work. Because damnit, I can't picture my life without you in it."

Her eyes sparkled with unshed tears as she smiled, her expression a mixture of tentative relief and hope.

What they had was real – something honest, something true. And while he knew there would be obstacles to overcome, he was ready to face them head-on, hand in hand with the woman who had captured his heart once more. He trusted her, more than he ever thought he could trust anyone. It was like some cosmic joke in the universe – here he was, standing in front of the woman who had hurt him beyond measure, yet he couldn't stop loving her with a depth that threatened to burn him alive.

"Okay," Emma breathed, a small smile tugging at the corners of her lips. "We're doing this. For real." She paused and inspected him again, that same compassionate look on her face as her hands brushed invisible lint off his lapels. "You've come a long way from the guy who used to throw tantrums on the football field."

"Hey now," Kyle shot back, his own grin quirking up at the edges. "I seem to recall you getting just as feisty back at home after the games."

"Well, I didn't like to see you hurt." She gave a delicate sniff and raised her nose in the air.

He couldn't stop himself.

Kyle swooped in for a gentle, lingering kiss that showed just how much he missed her. As it grew, the passion evolved to understanding and tenderness. It was a balm for his soul.

As they pulled reluctantly away, Kyle bent his neck so their foreheads could rest together. One of the perks of having a tall wife...ex-wife...maybe future wife again.

He smiled and closed his eyes, memorizing the sensation.

Kyle could still feel the ghost of her lips against his, the taste of her lingering on his tongue.

His phone rang in the other room for the umpteenth time, the shrill sound snapping him back to reality. "I have to get to the event," he groaned out, his voice tinged with regret.

Apparently his publicist had noticed that he wasn't on the line and decided to hang up and call again.

"Go," Emma whispered, offering him a small smile. "I'll be there soon, I promise."

He trailed his fingers over Emma's cheek one last time before he turned to leave. The warmth of her skin seemed to linger on his fingertips, and he squeezed his fist tight, wishing he could keep that tingle forever. He'd gone too many years without it.

"All right," he agreed, stealing one last look into her eyes before stepping back.

"Wait," she called out suddenly, causing him to pause at the door. "You've got...uh..." Emma motioned towards her own lips, her cheeks flushing with embarrassment. "Lipstick."

"Ah, the hazards of kissing a beautiful woman." Kyle grinned, wiping his mouth with the back of his hand. "Thanks for the heads-up."

"Anytime," she replied, her eyes twinkling with amusement. "Now go, before your publicist has a meltdown."

"See you soon, Em," he said, his chest light for the first time in years.

As he headed down the hallway, Kyle felt a sense of anticipation building within him. Tonight, would be the start of a new chapter in their lives – one where they would leave the past behind and move forward together. And no matter what challenges lay ahead, he knew they would face them together, ready to conquer whatever life threw their way.

He went to the room and with an exasperated sigh, unwillingly picked up his phone and answered. His tone, sharp and impatient, "I'm on my way, okay? Just hold on."

Sure, he had walked out minutes ago while his publicist was still prattling on, but he didn't think the guy would notice.

He really needed to hire Liam's publicist – that chick was a firecracker.

As he made his way to the event hall, his thoughts were already on Emma, on the night ahead, and on the promise of a future that felt brighter than ever before. He grinned at the thought of finally showing off the woman who had captured his heart so long ago.

Kyle envisioned her on his arm at tonight's event, radiant in the spotlight like she should have been eleven years prior. He could almost hear the hushed whispers and envious murmurs of onlookers as they made their grand entrance: the perfect couple reunited at last.

About damn time.

CHAPTER TWENTY

October 14, Friday
Emma

Twenty minutes later, Emma stood in front of the mirror, staring at herself in horror as her phone was pushed tight against her ear.

Dr. Thompson's voice held a note of genuine concern as she wrapped up her phone call. "Remember, you've faced this challenge before, and you're incredibly strong. We're here to fight this together and cancer treatments have come a long way since your last experience. We have a wider range of options available now than we did even a decade ago. We'll find the best plan for you. You're not alone."

Silence hung in the air, heavy and suffocating, as Emma still struggled to absorb the devastating confirmation. Tears welled up in her eyes, but she fought to maintain her composure. She didn't need to discuss this now. She needed to get ready. For Kyle.

For maybe the last time.

"Thank you for staying late so you could get me the results, Dr. Thompson," she managed to say, her voice quivering. "I...I appreciate it."

Dr. Thompson's response was tender with empathy. "Emma, I want you to understand that we'll explore all available treatment options. We're here for you, every step of the way."

"I know, and I...I appreciate that. I just...I'll see you next week at the follow-up," Emma choked out. She needed to get off the phone immediately or she'd break down so completely that she'd be late for the awards ceremony. She didn't want Kyle to start to worry about where she was.

The call ended, leaving Emma alone with the harsh reality of her situation. She took a deep, shuddering breath. Her hands weren't working right and her body wouldn't stop shaking.

What the heck was she supposed to do now?

Open the flood gates and let herself grieve and cry?

Or keep them tightly closed, in the fear that she'd never be able to close them again. She couldn't risk missing yet another important night for Kyle.

Kyle.

Ugh. Her attentive, sweet, protective Kyle. How was she supposed to tell him about this? And when?

Was she just supposed to go to the awards night and pretend nothing was wrong? Was she that good of an actress?

He'd wanted honesty, but could she give him that. Should she?

Should she just call Kyle and tell him the news and ruin another big night for him?

No.

Absolutely not.

Curling up and crying sounded like the best option, but...

He was counting on her.

He wanted her there. And damnit, he deserved it. He waited a decade to have her by his side at an event like this. He made it clear that it meant everything to him.

She inhaled unsteadily.

Okay, stuff it all in and process later. She always loved Elsa.

As a distraction, she forced herself to hum *Let It Go*, as loud as she could as she meticulously applied the finishing touches to her makeup. Everything tonight was going to be waterproof.

Just in case.

The bright lights from the vanity highlighted the turmoil and angst swirling in her eyes.

Emma was hoping only she could see it haunting her and that Kyle wouldn't notice, at least not at the party.

She tried to focus instead on how his strong arms would feel wrapped around her tonight, his warm breath on her neck, and those intense brown eyes locked onto hers. Despite her terrible news, she couldn't help but feel a small surge of anticipation for their evening together.

She had waited eleven years for this too, after all.

"All right, Emma, focus," she whispered to herself, trying to shake the distracting thoughts from her mind. "You've got this."

She was putting on her favorite pair of heels when a loud crash resonated from the kitchen. Emma froze, her heart leaping into her throat. A wave of unease washed over her, and she strained her ears, listening for any further noises. Had Duncan been released from jail and no one told her? Who would have posted his bail?

The only thing she could hear, now, were her own ragged breaths.

Get it together, Em.

Something must have just been stacked funny and fell.

Gravity: can't live with it, can't live without it.

It was just gravity.

The psycho stalker had been caught.

It was gravity...

But the nagging sensation that something was wrong persisted, and curiosity ultimately won out.

Curiosity killed the cat. She bit her lip and hesitated before slowly leaving her room, her head checking both sides of the hallway before venturing out.

Creeping towards the kitchen, she took slow, cautious steps, her pulse pounding in her ears.

It was something falling. That was all...

But the icy tendrils of fear continued to wrap around her heart, tightening their grip with each step closer.

As Emma entered the kitchen, her breath caught in her throat. The once pristine room now resembled a war zone. Deep red paint was splattered everywhere. The similarities to blood spatter scenes in her favorite crime shows had her choking back a cry of alarm.

Her body was frozen, but her eyes moved frantically around the room, looking for the person who did this. She strained so hard to hear a noise that she started to pick up the sounds of her own pulse.

It was then that she noticed a chilling detail amidst the chaos – a old photograph of her and Kyle had been viciously vandalized, their faces scratched out with a sharp object.

She was glued to the spot.

The police had caught someone.

But they sure as heck didn't catch the *right* someone.

The thought sent shivers down her spine.

Emma tried to maintain her composure despite the mounting panic.

Get safe. Call the police. Call Kyle.

In that order.

The eerie silence was shattered by the sound of footsteps echoing from the living room. Emma's pulse quickened, her breaths shallow and ragged as she tried to steady herself. She strained her ears, hoping it was just her imagination playing tricks on her. That the culprit had just made a scene and left again, rather than sticking around...

But the sound of footfall continued, drawing nearer.

"Who's there?" she called out, her voice trembling with fear. No response came, but the footsteps grew closer. Every instinct screamed at her to run, to escape this nightmare and never look back. But instead, she found herself rooted to the spot, unable to tear her gaze away from the doorway that led to the living room.

You've faced worse than this. You fought cancer, for God's sake. You can handle some stranger in your house. Get a knife from the block on the counter!

Her thoughts were demanding but her body refused to move.

The footsteps stopped abruptly, and Emma felt a chill run down her spine as she stared at the opening leading to the living room. The person must be waiting around the corner.

Damn her for buying a house with two entrances to the living room!

Her heart pounded in her chest, a wild, desperate rhythm that threatened to consume her. She couldn't help but envision all the terrible things that might be waiting for her – a sadistic killer, a deranged stalker...or perhaps something even worse.

As her thoughts spiraled into darker territory, a soft, almost gentle voice cut through the silence. "Hello, Emma."

Emma whirled around, dropping her phone, startled by the unexpected greeting. There, standing just a few feet away, was a woman with dark hair and piercing green eyes. She was dressed casually, as if she belonged in the house, but her smile held a sinister edge that made the hairs on the back of Emma's neck stand up.

Finally, her feet decided to listen, and she frantically walked backwards, not taking her eyes off the woman in front of her.

"Who are you?" Emma choked out. "What do you want?"

Her right foot slipped a little in the red paint and she hastily caught herself by placing her hands on the counter, now covering her hands in paint as well. She shuffled backward as the woman stepped closer.

If Emma could keep the island between them, maybe she could reach the knife block in time.

"Isn't it obvious?" The woman's tone was coy, her eyes sparkling with a twisted delight as she took in Emma's fear. "I want you to see what happens when you mess with things that don't belong to you."

"What?"

"Ah, I'm disappointed. The characters in your books are always so quippy and clever. And here you are...the opposite. I should have known you were a fraud – that's on me." The woman sighed tiredly, stepping closer. "But I'm afraid you're going to learn the hard way...that you can't always get what you want."

And with that chilling declaration, the pursuit began.

"Listen, I don't know who you are or what your problem is, but you need to leave. Now." Emma's voice shook as she backed another step.

She'd have to turn her back to get the knife block, so she had to be quick...

"Or what, Emma?" the woman sneered, her grin widening. "You'll call the police? Face it, sweetheart – you're outmatched and outplayed. And I've only just begun."

As the woman advanced, Emma's world began to close in around her. The walls seemed to be converging, suffocating her, trapping her in a never-ending cycle of dread. She knew she had to act, had to find a way to break free from this madwoman's clutches before it was too late.

The woman rounded the corner of the island and was now directly in front of her. Emma needed to act. Either she turned and grabbed for a knife...or she continued shuffling around the island and could try to sprint for the front door...

"Please, just stop. Just wait a minute," Emma said while raising her shaking hands up between them like a barrier. Emma's eyes darted around the room for anything she could use as a weapon. "Just tell me how I hurt you. I'll make it right, I promise. Just...stop moving!" She ended on a yell when the woman didn't stop her slow prowl towards her.

The woman stopped and cocked her head at Emma. "You haven't pieced the clues together yet, Miss Mystery author? Tsk tsk. I'm disappointed. I'll help. Nice to finally meet you. I'm Jaz."

Jaz? Who the fuck was Jaz?

The confusion showed on her face and the woman's face darkened with rage.

"Jaz!" She screamed. "I'm Jaz!" A vein on her forehead popped and her face turned brutally red.

Oh crap.

Emma skirted around the island; she needed space between them. Stat.

"I'm Kyle's Jaz!" Jaz screamed again, taking another fast few steps forward and Emma continuing shuffling.

Kyle's Jaz?

Oh.

Her stomach squeezed.

Oh.

Another few steps and Emma would be back at the knife block...

A second chance.

How long could they do this? The paint was slippery as hell, though the madwoman didn't seem bothered by it.

"Fine. You want me to stay away from Kyle? I will. Just let me go."

"Nice try, Emma. But I think we both know it can't be that easy. You broke him. Hurt him beyond repair. Even now you're toying with him. You need to be punished."

Should Emma agree that she was toying with Kyle to pacify the woman? Or should she deny it and play up the fact they had a common ground of shared love for Kyle?

Her heart would slow down long enough for her to think it out.

"You broke him. And now I'm going to fix him." Jaz reached behind her and pulled a long knife out of her waistband...

The very knife that Emma's right hand was running around the countertop, trying to find.

Jaz gave her a twisted smile. "I'm going to fix him and prove I'm the one who loves him more than anyone – more than *you* ever could."

"By breaking into houses and terrorizing us?"

She took a deep breath, trying to steady her racing thoughts. Clearly the knife was an escalation...what else did Emma have in the house that she could use?

"See, you don't even deny it. I knew you didn't love him." Jasmin's eyes shone bright, too bright. "I've seen the way you look at him, pretending you care. But deep down, we both know the truth – you'll always be the same selfish girl who broke his heart."

Emma's foot slipped again in the paint and she darted a glance at the door. She could try to run to it, but she might slip and it would leave her exposed. And with her hands as covered in paint as they were...would she be able to get the door open and out of it before Jaz could catch up?

"Kyle deserves better than you, Emma," Jaz spat, taking another menacing step. Her erratic movements were like a viper, coiling and ready to strike. "He deserves someone who won't abandon him when things get tough. Someone who won't break his heart." She waved her arm and Emma's eyes caught on the marks in her elbow.

Oh. Maybe that's how she knew Duncan...

That must be a new thing – there was no way Kyle would be involved with someone like that...

"Let's see how long you walk in circles, Emma. It's cute you still think you have a chance, especially in that form hugging dress that offers no give or flexibility." Jaz purred, her eyes narrowing dangerously. "I like that you have hope. So that way, I can break it, just like you broke Kyle's ability to trust and love. But trust *me* when I say, by the time I'm done with you, you'll be begging for mercy."

The sound of Jaz's deranged laughter echoed through the room, sending a chill down Emma's spine. Her eyes darted around the kitchen again, searching for something – anything – to use as a weapon if necessary. Jaz continued to circle her like a predator, her movements fluid and dangerous.

"Kyle can't love me because of what you've done to him. You broke his heart, left him when he needed you most. And now, even though you're back in his life, you still hold this power over him – keeping him from truly being happy with me." Jaz said, her voice dripping with poison. Then, she lunged toward Emma with an unexpected burst of speed.

Emma barely had time to react, her body moving on instinct as she sidestepped Jaz's attack and scrambled around the island.

"Face it, Emma," Jaz taunted, now randomly making sharp movements toward Emma like she was going to lunge for her again. The false lunges had Emma slipping even more on the wet floor as panic really started to set in. "You're nothing but a burden on Kyle – a constant reminder of pain and heartbreak. And until you're gone from his life completely, he'll never be able to move on."

Jaz circled, her eyes cold and calculating. "You know, I've learned quite a bit about you and Kyle," she said, her voice dripping with malice. "For instance, did you know that he still keeps your wedding ring in his sock drawer?" She paused, letting the information sink in. "I bet it eats away at him every day, thinking of how you betrayed him all those years ago. Right after we broke up, I did what any good lover would do and researched him some more so we could see a therapist together. Work through his issues so he could allow himself to love me. I wanted to know what to bring up so we could find a way to heal his trauma. I knew it had something to do with an ex-wife...I just had no clue that it was going to be you! Go figure. My favorite author breaks the heart of the love of my life. So, sorry, babe. It was either you or him. And unlike your stupid ass, I choose him."

"Tell me what you want. Just tell me. I'll do anything," Emma said through chattering teeth, fighting to keep her voice steady. "What do you want from me?"

"Ah, now we're getting somewhere," Jaz said, an unsettling smile spreading across her face. She pointed at the phone that Emma had dropped with a manicured finger. "I want you to call Kyle and break up with him."

That was it?

Sure.

Kyle would be all for that plan especially if it kept her alive. He'd be able to tell something was wrong and be able to rush home. He'd be able to stop this.

"Yes, okay! Yes. Just give me the phone!" Her eagerness had the woman's eyes narrowing on her.

"No, dear Emma. It's not that simple. There's a price to this trade. One I'm not so sure you're going to be so eager to pay."

Another step toward Emma, and another shuffle and slip away.

"You will call him," Jaz ordered, her eyes narrowing dangerously. "Tell him it's over. Make him understand that he deserves better than you and you'll remind him that he's not right for you." The woman paused and her eyes gleamed maniacally. "But first...first, you need to pay the toll for phone privileges. I did promise to make you hurt like you hurt him."

With those chilling words, Jaz lunged at Emma, who slipped and couldn't dodge the knife swipe. She cried out as it lashed across her arms and back.

Another swipe.

And another.

As hard as she tried to get up off the floor and away from the slicing blade, she was no match for Jaz's relentless assault.

Emma could feel the weight of every breath, each one heavier than the last, knowing that if she didn't act soon, she would never see Kyle again. Emma turned her head as she used all fours to slosh through the paint to slow the ongoing attacks.

"Did you really think you could replace me, Emma?" Jaz spat, her eyes wild and manic. "Did you really believe that Kyle could ever love you the way he loved me? But don't worry, I'll make sure he knows exactly who he should be with."

In a flash, Jaz's hand shot out again, grazing her forehead and cheek. On the very spots that Kyle's fingers had traced so lovingly earlier that evening. The pain seared through her, making her gasp as she stumbled backward onto her side. The wet paint clung to her butt and legs of the dress.

"Stop!" Emma pleaded, her voice raw with desperation. "Please, Jaz, don't do this!"

"Stop? Like you stopped loving Kyle? You destroyed him so thoroughly that a couple weeks ago when he saw *you* in the diner he stormed right by me and didn't even *see me*! He was so consumed with *you* that he walked right by *me* like I was a *stranger*! Like I was *nobody*!" Her shriek of agony caused Emma to wince. "I knew his damage was much deeper than I thought. A few phone calls and letters weren't going to solve the problem. I needed to step it up if I was going to save him. So, now, you need to do one little thing to help him get closure, and then we're going to play for a little bit. Then, after I feel like you've suffered enough...you'll be free."

Free? Like...from life? Or from her?

Jaz was beyond reason, consumed by an obsession that had driven her to madness. As Emma tried to scramble away, Jaz closed in, her eyes alight with a terrible, manic glee.

"Get ready to say goodbye to your precious love story, Emma," Jaz whispered, her voice cold and devoid of any humanity.

Emma saw a flash of silver and felt the knife's razor edge pierce deep into her skin.

CHAPTER TWENTY-ONE

October 14, Friday
Kyle

Kyle stood amidst the lavish décor of the Springfield Spartans' award banquet, his eyes constantly darting towards the entrance.

He was a bundle of nerves, fingers tapping impatiently against his glass of water as he eagerly awaited Emma's arrival. The room buzzed with chatter, laughter and the clinking of glasses, but all he could focus on was the nagging worry that gnawed at him with each passing minute.

Where was Emma?

He tried to ignore the sinking feeling in his chest.

As the evening progressed, his anxiety grew. He couldn't shake the feeling that something was wrong. At their shared table, his teammates noticed his restlessness and exchanged concerned glances.

Liam, one of his closest friends on the team, leaned in and asked, "Yo, everything okay? You seem...off."

Kyle sighed, running a hand through his hair. "I'm just waiting for Emma. She said she'd be here, but she's running late." He couldn't hide the note of concern.

Jen, who was perched in John's lap while he was whispering intently with Danny, whipped around to face Kyle, inspecting him closely.

"Yeah, I haven't had time to catch up with her much this week besides random texts, what with the whole stalker situation and all. How is she?"

"She's good, still waiting for the other shoe to drop, I think. I don't remember her being so cautious about things." He trailed off as he watched Jen's face turn carefully blank.

What was that?

"So, she's back at her house, but is still coming tonight?" She squinted at him. "And you're looking forward to her presence?"

Oh.

That was her angle.

The guys at the table were now paying attention, too. Thankfully, most of their ladies were off somewhere else, so it wasn't quite like facing a firing squad.

Though it was pretty damn close.

Kyle cleared his throat and leveled a look at Jen. "We're starting over. Fresh. We've reconciled and moved past our prior decisions. We've promised to be honest and forthcoming from here on out. We're good. Moving on."

His announcement hung in the air, and the guys at the table seemed to hold their breath for a moment before they erupted into cheers and congratulations.

Jen raised an immaculately arched eyebrow as she continued to study him closely, her lips pinched tight. "Really? How did that happen?"

Confusion caused his back to tighten.

"Long story," Kyle replied with a dismissive shrug. "We talked things out. Bared our souls. Decided to trust each other and move forward. All that jazz."

Jen was still inspecting him like she would a bug. "And you're...okay?"

What did that mean?

He cocked his head at her and she mirrored the movement.

"Stop giving him shit, Jen. He's happy and they've moved on. Stop poking the bear." John gave her a little shake and a quick kiss to her shoulder as she remained perched on his lap.

Jen didn't respond, just maintained her eye contact with Kyle with narrowed eyes.

Fuck. Did she expect a formal apology written in the sky for him ever being a douche to Emma?

Just as he was about to tell her to back off, his phone vibrated in his pocket. He pulled it out and saw Emma's name on the screen.

Finally!

"Hey, where are you?" Damn, he sounded like his publicist now.

Emma's voice trembled, and she sounded like she had been crying. "Kyle, I'm so sorry, but I can't do this."

Kyle's heart stopped. "What? Why? What happened? Are you okay?"

She sucked in a sharp breath. "I've just had some time to think about things, and I just can't do this, Kyle. I wanted so badly to make it work and pretend everything was okay. But it's not. You know it's not. It would never work between us. We're just too different. I don't know what I was thinking." She let out a pained whimper.

Kyle pushed from his seat and took two steps away from the table, his hands starting to shake as his grip on the phone tightened. "Emma, what the hell are you talking about? We're perfect together. Hell, even when I hated you, I couldn't stop loving you."

A sound like a painful mew came through the phone. "Kyle..."

"What's going on? The truth."

"Kyle. Kyle, I'm sorry, but I tried. I just...want to love you. But I can't. You're overwhelming and suffocating, and you bombard me with endless waves of emotions. I wanted to love you desperately, but it's just not meant to be. You're just too loud. Too temperamental. You have too many big feelings; it exhausts me. I can't handle them, and I don't want to. I wanted so bad to love you, but it's just not going to work. The future is just too uncertain. I don't want to just tackle today, I want to plan for tomorrow's tackle, and the tackle after that, and the game after that. And the future with you is just too uncertain." She ended verbal assault on a sob.

Each word fell like stones dropping into an already dry well, stirring up nothing but feelings of regret and self-loathing.

Of course.

Of course, she would do this again. Why did he think this time would be any different?

He'd hand it to her, she'd tricked him *good*.

"You win." He bent his neck to stare at his shoes and tried to smother the burn he felt growing in his sinuses. "You don't have to love me, but can you at least drag yourself here and pretend to be supportive? Just so I can accept my award and then you can leave? Then, I'll never ask you for anything else again. I promise. I just...even though you don't want to be here, *I* still want you here."

Shit, he was fucked in the head.

Emma's voice trembled as she continued quietly. Brokenly. "I don't care about your stupid award, Kyle."

What the hell was this?

"Emma, what the hell is going on?"

Emma's words were choked with her cries and barely distinguishable. But he did manage to discern two sentences: "This isn't going to work. I can't handle this."

Kyle's temper spiked but as Emma continued to sob and mumble inconsolably, that white-hot anger dissipated as easily as it arose. Now, he felt nothing but a vast desert of emptiness.

"Fine." He sighed.

He just couldn't summon the will to be angry. Not anymore. A man could only take so much heartbreak before his system just...stopped working.

"Have a great life, Emma."

Kyle pulled his phone from his ear and squeezed it hard in his fist, willing himself not to roar out his pain. He dragged his body around to face his friends who were staring with wide, concerned eyes.

Eavesdroppers.

He lowered himself into his chair, moving slowly so his body wouldn't shatter.

How could she still hold this power over him?

Why did he not learn?

Why had he let her in again?

He placed his phone down on the table with controlled movements. His hands shook with rage and hurt, and he tried to steady himself by taking slow, deep breaths.

"Everything okay?" Jen asked.

Fucking glorious – what did it fucking look like?

He settled on, "Emma's not coming."

"Why not?" John asked.

"Apparently, we're not a good fit and tomorrow is an unknown."

"Kyle, I—" Jen started, but he cut her off with a sharp gesture.

"Save it, Jen. Just...save it."

His mind raced as he fought to make sense of the whirlwind of emotions battering him from all sides. Betrayal, confusion, and pain twisted together until he couldn't tell where one ended and the other began. And beneath it all, a single question echoed through his head: Why?

Kyle struggled to hold himself together. Shortly, they'd be starting the awards, and he was supposed to go up there and smile and act like his world hadn't just crumbled to pieces. Again.

"Damn, man. Sorry to hear that," Liam said, clapping him on the back, while others murmured their sympathies.

"Thanks," Kyle muttered, forcing a small chuckle. "Guess some things just aren't meant to be."

As everyone went back to their conversations and drinks, Kyle's thoughts turned inward, replaying the phone call and searching for clues. What had changed in the past few hours? Why had Emma decided to break up with him now, of all times?

"Kyle," Jen's voice interrupted his thoughts. Her dark eyes were filled with concern as she slid off John's lap and grabbed the chair next to him. She leaned close. "Did Emma say anything about getting a call from her doctor?"

"What?" Kyle blinked, caught off guard by the question. "No, she didn't mention anything like that."

"Shit." Jen bit her lip, worry etched across her face. "I was just wondering if maybe the cancer was back and that's why she was panicking." Jen's shoulders slumped. "I guess not," she mumbled, her brow wrinkled with confusion and disappointment.

His entire body stiffened and stared at Jen. The blood drained from his face as he comprehended her words, his heart sinking to the pit of his stomach like a lead weight.

"What did you say?"

Jen looked up from the floor and tilted her head at him, quizzically.

"I just wanted to know if the cancer came back...the last I heard she was still waiting for results. So, I was wondering..." She slowly stopped speaking, promoted into silence by the look on his face.

"What do you mean, if the cancer came back?" Kyle felt rooted to the spot, as though any movement would cause him to shatter into a million pieces. He swallowed hard, terror washing over him like an icy wave. His grip tightened on the table as he tried to process what she'd just said.

"I, uh..." Jen looked around and found nothing but dark, worried expressions staring back at her.

"Kyle, you said you guys cleared the air...and discussed everything." She gave him a horrified look. "You said you guys were *honest*!" She ended it on a semi-shriek that caused guests of the gala to turn and look their way.

"Yeah, we said we'd be honest going forward and we'd talk about why she ripped my heart out years ago with no warning..."

Oh, fucking god. Oh, God. No.

He stared at Jen in horror, his body not working right.

Cancer?

His Emma had cancer?

Or...still had it?

"Fuck," Kyle repeated, his anger quelled by a sickening wave of concern. "Oh fuck." He fought off a wave of nausea. "Why didn't she tell me?"

"She said she didn't want to worry you over a silly scare," Jen said, her voice now full of guilt and reluctance. "She didn't know how you'd handle it."

"Damnit!" Kyle slammed his fist on the table, making several teammates jump. "Fucking hell! I can't believe I didn't see it." He stared at the floor, guilt gnawing at him as he remembered the pain in Emma's voice.

He should have known. He should have seen the signs. Emma had always been so strong, so independent, and so fiercely private. But now, looking back, he could see everything so clearly. The fatigue, the weight loss, the sudden breakup. It had all been right there in front of him, and he had been too blind to see it.

Hell, even now. Her obsession with organic food, her castor oil wraps and detoxes, her sauna visits, and ice baths.

Kyle couldn't believe he had been so clueless.

While he was busy fighting for his football career, Emma had been *fighting for her life.*

Alone.

The guilt he felt was crushing him. He had let her down. He had abandoned her when she needed him the most.

"I need to go see her," Kyle said, standing up from the table. "Can you track down William for me and let him know I had an emergency?"

Jen nodded and stood with him. "Be careful," she said, her voice soft with concern. "She's been through a lot."

"Well, now that I know what I'm dealing with, I'm a bit more fucking prepared."

He still couldn't believe that she'd never told him. Back then...or today.

They'd been living together for a few weeks and she never mentioned a word.

All this time, struggling alone.

His heart squeezed.

He looked at Jen and lowered his voice. "This is what it was? What caused her to ask for a divorce?"

He didn't need her to confirm, but still...

Jen sighed heavily and nodded, her eyes filled with guilt. "She didn't want you to worry or be distracted from your career. She thought she was doing what was best for you."

Kyle's jaw clenched as the weight of the revelation settled in. He could feel his heart pounding against his ribcage, a mixture of anger and sorrow coursing through him. "So, she's been dealing with this all by herself...all these years?"

"You know Emma. Even though she's quiet, she's protective of those she loves. Probably too much for her own good," Jen said, her voice tinged with concern.

"And I've been pissed at her for leaving me, not knowing she was fighting for her life." Kyle ran a hand through his hair, his frustration at himself and the situation evident. "Why didn't she fucking tell me?"

"You know why," Jen said, placing a comforting hand on his shoulder. "She thought she was saving you."

"Fuck..." Kyle muttered, his gaze dropping to the floor as he struggled to process the information. He felt like a complete idiot for not recognizing the signs sooner. The weight of guilt and distress threatened to suffocate him. "I should have been there for her, then and now. Instead, I was just...angry. And awful to her."

"Kyle, listen to me," Jen said firmly, making him look up at her. "Now is not the time for self-pity or guilt. Emma needs you. You need to go find her and be there for her, no matter what. Or, if you can't, then call me and the girls, and we will be."

"No. It will be me. It will always be me. And then, once we know she's okay, I'm going to chew her ass the fuck out for stripping that decision from me and making herself go through that alone."

"Well, at least you have a plan," Jen gave him a supportive push toward the exit. "And remember, Kyle, she loves you. She just needs to know you're there for her. So, maybe don't chew her out quite yet."

As Kyle made his way through the crowd, heading for the door, he couldn't help but replay the recent phone call with Emma in his head. All the anger he'd felt was misplaced, replaced by an overwhelming sense of urgency to find her and make things right.

The crisp evening air hit him like a slap in the face as he burst through the doors of the event hall, but he barely felt it. He sprinted to his car, fumbling for his keys as he fought to keep his panic at bay.

Kyle got into his car and started the engine, his mind racing with thoughts of Emma. He couldn't bear the thought of her going through cancer treatment all by herself. It was a cruel and unjust thing for anyone to have to endure. But for Emma? His Emma?

Unconscionable.

What was it like years ago to go through that alone?

His heart hurt just thinking about it.

"Fuck, I've been such an idiot," he muttered under his breath, shaking his head in disbelief.

What would he find when he got back to her place?

Would he find Emma broken, sobbing uncontrollably? Would she be stoic, trying to keep up her strong, independent façade? Or would she be straight up *gone*? Once again packed up and vanished...

With tires screeching, he sped off toward her home, his thoughts consumed by worry for Emma's well-being.

As he raced through the city streets, he couldn't help but berate himself for his blindness. How could he have missed the signs? The exhaustion, the quiet moments when she'd retreat into herself, the way she'd sometimes avoid his gaze when they talked about the future.

His mind raced back to their past, and he wished he could have been there for her through her darkest times. But now, he had a chance to make things right, and he wasn't going to let that opportunity slip away.

"Please, Emma," he whispered, his voice heavy with emotion. "Please be okay."

Kyle's car screeched to a halt in her driveway, the tires leaving dark streaks on the pavement.

His gaze shifted to the familiar car parked haphazardly in the driveway, blocking in Emma's small car, and his stomach tightened.

What the fuck was Jaz doing here?

Of all the nights for his ex to show up, it had to be this one. She better not be bothering Emma, especially if Emma needed space to process the news from her doctor.

His pulse thundered in his ears as he realized the window next to the front door was shattered, glass shards glinting like tiny daggers in the moonlight.

"Oh fuck."

He tried to push down the dread bubbling up inside him that was demanding that he sprint into the house with metaphorical guns blazing.

He swung open the car door and stepped out, making his way up to the door. His boots crunched on the broken glass as he approached the house.

His thoughts were a whirlwind of fear, anger, and confusion.

As he reached for the doorknob, he noticed the front door was hanging ajar.

Something was wrong.

Very wrong.

The house was eerily quiet, the silence amplifying his already heightened senses. The only sound he could hear from outside were his own shaky breaths.

His stomach twisted into knots, and he hesitated for a moment before pushing open the door.

CHAPTER TWENTY-TWO

October 14, Friday
Kyle

Rushing through the front door, he abruptly stopped, his eyes widening in shock as he took in the chilling sight that greeted him. The kitchen had been transformed into a chaotic mess, bathed in a sinister shade of deep red.

What sent shivers down his spine, even more than the unmistakable tracks smeared across the floor, narrating the gruesome events, was the overwhelming crimson hue that now enveloped Emma. It was chillingly clear; this red was one hundred percent real, and it wasn't all just paint.

"Emma!" he breathed, his voice cracking.

The love of his life was bound to a chair in her kitchen, her once pristine outfit now torn and bloody. Her long hair was a wild mess, framing her glossy and confused blue eyes that stared at him in desperation as she sagged against the ropes that held her up. She was already bruised and had one eye that would be swollen completely shut shortly, as well as numerous cuts on her half-painted body.

Jaz stood over her, caressing a bloody knife against her cheek.

Kyle's heart stopped beating.

"Stay back, Kyle," Jaz warned, her eyes never leaving Emma's limp form. A baseball bat lay discarded by her feet. "I'm helping you find closure."

Holy fucking shit.

When he broke up with her, he told her that a woman from his past burned him bad and he didn't want to get committed because he wasn't healed from it yet.

Really it was because she was getting creepily clingy, and he wasn't interested in putting up her any longer.

Holy fuck. *He* did this. *He* caused this.

Kyle's mind raced, searching for any way to defuse the situation and save Emma from this madwoman.

"Jaz, please," he began, his voice thrumming with emotion. "Let her go. We can figure this out."

"Figure this out?" Jaz laughed maniacally. "You think I don't know you still love her? It's okay, Jaz." She started talking to herself. "She'll be out of the way soon, and then we can finally be together."

"Jaz, please, let's talk about this," Kyle implored, his voice trembling as he tried to reason with the deranged woman. Her wild eyes flickered between him and Emma, her grip tightening on the bloody knife.

"Kyle, don't you see? This is our chance to be together!" Jaz exclaimed, her tone distressingly manic. "She'll be out of the picture. We can finally move on and start our life together!"

"Jaz...you don't want to do this. You don't want to hurt Emma," Kyle said, struggling to keep his fear in check as he watched Jaz closely. He knew he had to tread carefully; one wrong move could seal Emma's fate.

"Of course, I don't want to hurt her," Jaz replied, her voice dripping with false affection. "But sometimes sacrifices have to be made for love."

With that, she leaned down and ran the tip of the knife almost lovingly along Emma's cheek, causing a thin line of blood to appear. Emma winced and kicked weakly against the pain. Kyle clenched his fists, his heart pounding in his chest as he fought the urge to charge at Jaz. Instead, he focused on keeping her attention on him.

"Jaz, look at me. We can work through my issues, but...I can't be with you while you're in jail for murder. Think for a moment. There has got to be a better way," he demanded, his voice filled with false confidence and authority. "Can't we make her pay in a different way? Hell, look at her. She's a fucking mess. Maybe she's already paid up."

He stilled when her forehead furrowed.

Shit, did he play it a little too hard?

She met his gaze, her expression momentarily softening before her eyes blazed with renewed fervor.

"See, Kyle?" she whispered, her voice shaky from adrenaline. "I'm doing this for us." The knife continued its cruel journey, tracing another shallow cut across Emma's neck.

Emma's eyes were wide with terror as the cold steel of the knife carved her skin, her chest heaving with ragged breaths.

Kyle's heart clenched painfully at the sight, fury and helplessness warring within him.

"Jaz," he tried again, forcing a steadiness into his voice that he didn't feel. "You don't want to do this. I promise you; we can work things out. Just let Emma go, and we'll figure it all out together."

"Really?" Jaz asked suspiciously, her grip on the knife tightening as she eyed Kyle warily. The blade hovered dangerously close to Emma's vulnerable eyes, and Kyle bit back a curse.

"Of course," he replied, his mind racing as he sought any way to defuse the situation. "We can go get help together, Jaz. We can work through this...brokenness in me with a professional. Let's do that. We'll see a therapist together. Fuck, it was probably my absentee mom, let's start by discussing her...but first, you need to let Emma go. Police involvement would prevent me from healing the way I should."

Jaz's wild eyes flickered between Kyle and Emma, indecision playing across her features for a moment before she snarled, "No. You're just saying that so I'll let her go! You don't really care about me!"

"Jaz, I swear, I'm not lying to you," Kyle insisted, hating himself for how easily the words came but recognizing that they might be his only chance to save Emma. "I want to get help and heal my broken heart. With you. But you need to put down the knife."

He shifted his feet and took a step closer. He needed to do something drastic – something Jaz wouldn't expect.

"Jaz, wait," Kyle said, his voice cracking as he dropped to his knees, hands raised in surrender. "I need to tell you something important."

Jaz hesitated, the hand with the knife lowering slightly as she eyed him cautiously. "What are you doing? No, get up Kyle, you'll get paint over your new suit. You just got that back from the dry cleaners this week."

Fuck, how did she know that?

Focus.

"Emma...that heartless bitch...she taught me how to love and lose, but it was *you* who healed me," Kyle began, pouring every ounce of sincerity he could muster into his words. "I need to close the chapter on Emma, but I can't get closure if she's dead."

She's a bookworm, use that.

"A romantic tragedy. A Romeo and Juliet story. I don't want my name to be associated with the dead author Emma Potter for all eternity. I want it to be linked...to you. As my wife."

His heart thundered in his chest as he prayed that she'd buy this performance.

"Please, Jaz, let her go. We can be together, just like we always wanted."

For a moment, Jaz seemed to consider his words, her wild eyes flicking between him and Emma. Then, as if weighing the decision, she lowered the knife and stared at Kyle, a triumphant smile playing at the corners of her lips.

"Really, Kyle?" she asked breathlessly, a hint of madness still lingering in her gaze. "You really choose me?"

"Of course, Jaz. Always. From here on out, I'll always choose you," he lied, trying extremely hard not to stare at Emma's rapidly drooping eyelids and increasingly heavy head.

Jaz rushed toward him, her face full of pure bliss.

Kyle used every ounce of muscle and skill that had been driven into him since middle school to thrust up from his semi-kneeling position. Using his legs, he pushed himself as hard as he could toward Jaz's approaching embrace. Instead of rising to a stand though, he stayed low.

The low man always wins.

With a decade's worth of experience, Kyle Justice speared the oncoming attacker right in her center, his shoulder driving into her stomach so hard that the knife in her grip clanged to the floor and she let out a winded scream as they sailed through the air and crashed into the island behind her.

CHAPTER TWENTY-THREE

October 14, Friday
Kyle

The force of the impact caused Kyle to take a second to catch his own breath.

After he regained some semblance of motor function, he leapt up and away from the still figure below him, ready to tackle the next thing she threw at him.

Instead, the woman lay still on the floor, unmoving.

Still breathing though.

Unfortunately.

Kyle ripped off his tie and flipped her over unceremoniously. As tight as he could, he tied her hands behind her back. Maybe she'd lose circulation and need to have her hands amputated.

The very hands that were now responsible for the future endless amounts of scars and trauma his Emma would have to face for the rest of her life.

Emma.

Kyle whipped around to attend to her, but he hesitated. Common sense chimed in finally and he charged to the alarm system on the wall and slammed his finger on the big red button. Immediately, he turned and rushed to her side. She was losing consciousness. The amount of red paint splashed all over her body was concealing where her injuries were.

He felt useless as he clumsily tried to untie her from the chair.

"Emma, honey, are you all right? Talk to me, baby," he asked breathlessly, his stomach filled with concern as he visually inspected her battered and bloody form.

A weak nod was all she could manage, but it was enough to send a surge of gratitude through Kyle.

"Kyle...you came," she whispered, her gaze filled with wonder and something more – something that made his heart flip uncomfortably in his chest.

"Always," he replied softly, finally managing to cut the rope with Jaz's discarded knife.

Emma's body fell forward and into his. He caught her in his arms and that was when the seriousness of her condition became evident.

"Emma, baby, I'm here," he called out as he cradled her, his voice cracking with anxiety. "Just hold on for me, okay?"

"Kyle..." Emma managed, her own voice weak and strained. Blood trickled from the shallow cuts on her face and her once vibrant blue eyes now appeared dull, clouded by pain.

"Shit, shit, shit," Kyle muttered under his breath, his hands shaking as he ran them over her body, looking for holes to plug. He tried to keep up a steady stream of reassurances, but every word felt hollow and false in his throat. "You're going to be fine, Em. Just stay with me, all right? I won't let anything happen to you."

"Always...so stubborn, aren't you?" Emma attempted a small, tired smile, her pale lips quivering ever so slightly. "Never could...resist playing the hero..."

"Damn right," Kyle retorted, choking back a sob. "And who better to save than the woman who taught me how to love and lose, huh?"

He felt a warm spot of fabric on her side and caught sight of the blood seeping through her torn clothing. Horror raced through him, like ice water in his veins. He knew he needed to act fast, but for a moment, he was paralyzed by fear.

"Em, where does it hurt most?" He asked urgently, trying to force himself to focus. "Talk to me. We'll get you through this, I promise." He raised his eyes and looked for something to push against her stab wound. The towels on the door to the dishwasher were drenched in paint. Maybe she had some in the drawers?

He'd have to leave her and that would take too long to find.

Frantically, he slipped out of his suit jacket and started using the fabric to offer pressure.

"Everywhere..." she whispered, her voice barely audible over the sound of their breathing. "But it's okay. If It wasn't this, it'd be the cancer, eventually."

He swallowed hard, her words striking him like a blow to the chest. Trust – something they'd both struggled with for so long, and now, in this terrifying moment, it was all that held them together.

"All right, Em," he said, determination replacing fear as he took a deep, steadying breath. "Everything is fine and I'm here now. Just stay with me, and we'll get through this. Together. Tackle today, right?"

His voice sounded too tight; he was going to make her worry.

And as sirens approached in the distance, he held her close, praying that she'd be tough enough to see them both through the darkness.

"Come on, Em, you're gonna be all right," Kyle pleaded as he ripped off half of his shirt sleeve to tie around one of the deeper cuts on her arm. "I'm not sure what to do in a world without you in it. Just hold on."

"Always my knight in shining armor," she murmured, her blue eyes growing glassy and distant. "Even after everything..."

"Tackle today, okay? We got this." He sobbed out. The tears started falling as Emma began to slip in and out of consciousness in his lap.

"Always," she mouthed back.

As the sirens grew louder, Kyle cradled Emma in his arms, desperately willing her to stay conscious. "Don't leave me again, Em," he begged, tears streaming down his face. "I love you too damn much."

"Love you...always..." Her eyes fluttered closed, and she fell limp in his embrace.

"Emma!" Panic surged through him, and for a moment, everything around him seemed to fade away. But as the sirens stopped and the sounds of approaching footsteps filled the air, Kyle clung to the hope that they still had a chance – that the universe wasn't *that* cruel.

CHAPTER TWENTY-FOUR

Epilogue: October 13, Friday
Emma

A year later

Emma dabbed concealer under eyes still shadowed from restless nights and hospital vigils. Her hands shook slightly, as much from anticipation as from the chill seeping into her bones. She eyed a rouge compact, wondering if a touch of color might restore some illusion of health and vitality. With a humorless chuckle, she set it aside. Who was she kidding? She had never been very good at makeup and there was a point, where if you kept messing with things, the results tended to look worse..

Better quit while she was ahead.

Emma wrapped the blanket more snugly around her shoulders, burrowing deep into the plushness of the thick threads. Chloe had gifted her the chunky hand-knit blanket when she started going through chemo again, so she'd have something to snuggle with in the chair as she waited. Emma loved weaving her fingers into the soft fabric so much that even now that she was done with the chemo treatments, she continued to bring it everywhere. Plus, she was cold all the time, now. She forgot how much warmth hair trapped on your head...when you had some. It got to the point that whenever she went to Jen for her now twice-weekly massages, Jen gifted her a special tote bag just to carry the blanket in so it wouldn't get dirty being toted from place to place. Jen called the bag *Emma's Tela Tote* – her fabric tote.

The doorbell interrupted her preparations, and Emma's heart skipped a beat.

Who would be knocking...Kyle was already with the guys, getting ready for the award night. Horrid flashbacks ripped through her and she swallowed hard before turning away from the mirror.

With care, Emma used a small, delicate scarf to protect her head from the evening's chill and tied it in a gentle knot to ensure it stayed snug.

Emma took slow steps toward the door, her phone in hand, just in case, and peeked through the eyehole. She let out a gasp and hurriedly pulled the door open to find all her friends, the girls, gathered on her doorstep.

"Surprise!" Jen, Julie, Chloe, Rose, Megan, Lexie, and Mia called out in various levels of exuberance. Mia was still relatively new to the crew, and was much more reserved compared to Jen and Lexie, but her excitement was palpable, nonetheless.

Emma's eyes widened and a smile bloomed across her face. "What are you nuts doing here!"

"Getting ready with you. Duh," Jen rolled her eyes before wrapping Emma in a fierce hug. The familiar scent of her coconut and lime and the warmth of her embrace chased away the evening's chill. "It's no fun getting ready solo."

"You didn't have to come all this way," Emma protested even as gratitude swelled within her.

"Nonsense," Chloe said while wrapping another knitted scarf around Emma's neck with a small hug and a peck on the cheek. "We need some calm to balance out Lexie's crazy. You're the perfect person to anchor us."

Emma blinked back tears, touched by their thoughtfulness. And complete BS.

"Now, are you going to make us stand out here all night, or are you going to invite us in?" Rose asks, a teasing glint in her eye. "I don't know about the rest of you, but I'm freezing!"

Laughter rippled through the group, and Emma quickly stepped back, ushering them inside. "Come in, come in! I'm so glad you're all here."

As all the girls pushed inside, the room filled with rich savory smells. Rose dragged in tote after tote filled with packaged food. Rose had become obsessed with healthy eating during her infertility treatments years before, and during Emma's cancer treatment, they bonded over their eating habits. Now, periodically, whenever Rose tried a new recipe, she'd make a double batch and bring some over for Emma and Kyle. They had to buy a chest freezer for all the meals that Rose gave them. Kyle suspected it was Rose's way of showing support during Emma's cancer treatment. He probably wasn't wrong.

"More? You just brought some by a couple days ago."

"Nonsense," Rose replied, brushing away Emma's protests. "You need to keep your strength up and you mentioned that you hated cooking when you felt sick. Now we can all snack as we get ready." Rose leaned in and shared her dirty secret. "Plus, I had leftovers from my food prep."

Emma smiled, seeing through Rose's casual tone. She knew how much work went into Rose's meal prep and how she always made extra for Emma's sake.

While Rose unpacked the food, Julie presented Emma with a gift bag. "A little something to celebrate your remission."

Emma peered inside and gasped at the sight of a silk robe and a set of luxurious pajamas in a soft watercolor blue. "Jules, you shouldn't have!" Emma exclaimed, tears blurring her vision. "This is too much." Julie was her ride to and from appointments whenever Kyle was out of town for games.

"Nah," Julie smiled and squeezed Emma's hand. "You'd do the same for any of us."

A lump formed in Emma's throat as she looked between her friends. After all the pain and uncertainty of the past year, their steadfast support was life changing.

She didn't know how she got through it all years ago when she didn't have them...or Kyle.

"Well, are we going to stand around all night or are we going to get ready?" Lexie barked out from the back of their circle, breaking the tension. In the bustle of activity, Emma almost forgot Lexie was there. Lex wasn't known for being quiet. Emma bit her lip when she realized Lexie had a knit cap pulled low over her head.

It was bound to happen.

With all the hair changes and crazy dye jobs that girl did, there was inevitably going to be a mishap.

But when Lexie pulled the cap from her head, Emma's heart stopped as she stared.

Lexie's crazy, colorful hair was gone, buzzed down to the scalp. The exact length of Emma's own fine, blond fuzz that was just starting to grow back in.

Tears blurred her vision as her eyes met Lexie's and gratitude swelled inside her chest. Emma rushed forward and threw her arms around Lexie, embracing her tightly.

"You didn't have to do this," Emma whispered.

"I know." Lexie's voice wavered. She allowed Emma to hug her tight for a minute before coughing gruffly. "But...I couldn't let you have all the attention; you know me."

Emma leaned back from her friend, tears slipping down her cheeks. Yes, she knew Lexie. And Lexie was all bark and no bite. This wasn't attention seeking. This was friendship, through and through.

The girls gathered around them, encircling them with their warmth and love. Emma's appreciation for their presence in her life threatened to overwhelm her.

After a long moment, they broke apart, laughter and chatter resuming. Emma felt Lexie's hand finding hers and squeezing tight. Emma gave her a watery smile and wiped her eyes.

The mood stabilized as Emma's friends descended upon her house like a whirlwind, their mingling and laughter dispelling the heaviness of the moment. The house was soon filled with joyful chaos as they all prepared for the evening ahead. Emma saw her reflection in the mirror and gave it a tentative smile, thinking for the first time, that the dark circles under her eyes maybe didn't seem so dark.

As Emma and Kyle's living room was transformed into a Sephora, cosmetics and beauty products strewn across every surface, the air was filled with competing fragrances from her friends' various perfumes.

Emma closed her eyes, breathed deep, and let the sounds of joyous friendship wash over her. However much longer her road may be, she wouldn't walk it alone.

She had friends.

And equally, if not more importantly, she had Kyle. She twirled her wedding bands absently as she basked in the moment.

When she opened her eyes again, she found Jen watching her, a soft smile on her face and understanding evident in her gaze.

Emma smiled back, feeling at peace.

Tackle today.

And heck, why not tackle tomorrow too.

Chapter Twenty-Five

Epilogue: October 13, Friday
Kyle

The golden light from the chandeliers cast a warm glow over the opulent ballroom as Kyle leaned back in his chair, a satisfied grin on his face. He scanned the table, taking in the familiar faces of his closest friends gathered around him, all dressed to impress for the annual awards night. The air was filled with the clatter of silverware, hearty huckles, and the hum of conversation.

"Man, can you believe we're here again?" Michael remarked, rubbing the back of his neck. "Feels like we were just doing this."

"Time flies when you're drowning in diapers," Kenny chimed in, raising his glass in a toast. "Here's to babysitters everywhere."

"Here, here!" Danny and Brandon chimed in.

The women were off somewhere, tormenting someone besides their men for a change. Except Emma. She sat beside Kyle, looking stunning in her elegant gown while patting at her head-wrap to make sure it was still secure. When she caught him looking, Emma gave him a playful wink, sending a shiver down his spine.

She was perfect. She was his. Forever. No takie-backsies. No matter how many times the cancer tried to come back – they'd kick its ass again and again.

Their evening was perfect. Good music, good food, and good company. What could be better? The friends shared stories and teased one another good-naturedly. Ryan recounted his latest disastrous date, while Michael and Liam debated the merits of different workout routines. It felt like a family gathering, each person bringing their own unique flair to the group.

As the evening progressed, William Galloway took the stage and gave his speech honoring and thanking the Spartan family for their contributions to people, places, and the planet. After a round of applause, William presented his award to Liam and gave him the stage for his own speech.

After his applause, Liam tapped his glass with a spoon, signaling for additional attention before he left the stage and the room returned to socializing.

The room quieted, all eyes turning toward him as he stood at the head of the stage.

"All right, everyone," Liam began. "It's that time of the evening. You know, the part where we get all sappy and emotional."

A ripple of laughter passed through the crowd, and Kyle shook his head in amusement. Trust Liam to keep things light-hearted.

"Seriously, though," Liam continued, his voice growing somber. "We're here tonight not only to celebrate our achievements on the field but also to honor the bonds we've formed off of it. The friendships, the support, the love – these are what make our team truly great."

Kyle felt a surge of pride as he listened to Liam's words. It had been a challenging year, but he knew he could always count on his friends to have his back. And with Emma by his side, life seemed more vibrant, more alive than ever before.

"I know we only do one per year and it's our honor to dedicate this night to that specific recipient every year for their outstanding character, works, and more..." Liam paused, taking a deep breath before continuing. "But this year, I want to invite a second person up." The few side whispers and conversations were now completely silent as well. "Kyle wasn't given a chance to formally receive his award last year and to receive the ovation that he clearly deserved."

Oh, holy shit.

As Liam finished his unexpected announcement, the room erupted into applause and cheers. Kyle blinked in shock for a moment before turning to Emma, who looked as stunned as he felt. Their gazes locked and it was as if they were the only two people in the room. Emma squeezed his hand, her eyes shining with pride and joy.

"Go," she whispered. "This is your moment. Finally. And I'm here for it." She gave him a wry smile.

Kyle leaned in and placed a quick but tender kiss on her lips, relishing in the familiar thrill of her touch.

"Thank you," he murmured against her mouth, knowing that without her love and strength, he wouldn't be standing here today.

He would have retired from football the second she started chemo, if she let him.

She wouldn't even hear it.

"Always," she replied with a soft smile, urging him towards the stage.

He let go of her hand reluctantly, feeling the warmth of her fingers lingering in his own. His stomach fluttered with nerves and excitement as he stood from the table, feeling the weight of everyone's gaze. With each step towards the stage, he thought about the journey that had led him to this moment – the triumphs and setbacks on and off the field, and most importantly, the love and support of the woman by his side.

Once on the stage, he faced the crowd, steeling himself for what he was going to say. As he leaned toward the mic, his vision was filled with friends, family, and countless others who had been there for him throughout the years.

Holy shit, that was a lot of people.

Why did this feel more overwhelming than a football game?

Probably because he didn't need to fucking *speak* at games.

Kyle cleared his throat, his gaze darting about, before locking eyes with Emma. She smiled up at him, her hands clasped at her chest, pride swimming in her eyes.

He felt a surge of love and gratitude that nearly took his breath away.

Emma. His sweet Emma.

Immediately, he knew what to say.

"Thank you," he began, his voice cracking with emotion. "I've waited a long time to give this speech – so let's hope it aged like a fine wine." He chuckled nervously but didn't break eye contact with Emma. "I wouldn't be here today if it wasn't for a girl in eighth grade, who was terrible at numbers, telling me that I could be anything I wanted to be. That girl became my best friend, my sometimes wife, and the center of my world. Emma, you believed in me when I couldn't even believe in myself. You are my heart, my soul, and my greatest love story."

Kyle raised his hand to his lips, blowing a kiss at Emma. It was a gesture he'd wanted to make for so long but had never been able to – until now. Then, he turned his attention back to the speech he had waited a decade for Emma to hear.

· · · ● · ● · ● · · ·

If you like my storytelling and think you'd enjoy *yummy* **hockey athletes** as well, take a look at my other series: **The Springfield Cyclones**

Hooking: A Steamy Bachelor Auction Hockey Romance – https://mybook.to/SCh

Discover More From Ella Haines

Springfield Spartans Standalone Romances:

Crystal Clear: A Steamy Springfield Stripper *Novella*

Offensive Holding: A Forbidden Friends-To-Lovers Stripper Romance *Novella*

Illegal Substitutions: A Friends-To-Lovers Steamy Sports Romance

Illegal Contact: A Steamy Sports Workplace Romance

Unsportsmanlike Conduct: A Steamy Single Mother Sports Romance

Intentional Grounding: A Steamy Opposites Attract Romance

False Start: A Steamy Second Chance Romance

Springfield Cyclones Standalone Hockey Romances:

Boarding: A Steamy Hockey Romance *Novelette*

Hooking: A Steamy Bachelor Auction Hockey Romance

Social Media Information - Ella Haines

Did you enjoy this book?

If so, please visit **www.EllaHaines.com** and sign up for the newsletter to receive additional scenes, freebies, and updates on future releases.

Newsletter signup here:
http://ellahaines.com/newsletter-for-freebies/

Also, if you have an eagle eye and caught any typos that slipped through the rounds and rounds of edits, take a moment and think if you'd like to be an ARC or beta reader for any future releases! If so, drop me an email! I'd love to have you on the team.

If you find any typos, you can let me know here: EllaHaines.author@gmail.com

About Author - Ella Haines

Ella Haines is a lover of all things love. Raised to know that she could be anything in the world, she made the wild and crazy decision to become a neurotic accountant. Balancing trial balances and filing taxes didn't quite fill her bucket, so she started dabbling in short stories. Those short stories evolved into complex storylines with empowered women, their families and friends, and the hunky men who adore them.

Request For Review

If this book brought you a smile and you think others might enjoy
it, please review it on your purchasing platform
(and copy it to Goodreads if you're willing and able).

This helps to spread the word about the book. Social proof to other
readers is important.

It also brings me joy <3

Praise For Ella Haines

"It kept me hooked with the angst and sweet moments" - Nicole, book review

"All the feels from the frustration, anger, pain and hurt that came flowing out from the never ending angsty-ness truly hit hard many times throughout. Putting you through the ultimate wringer in what was a super emotionally charged ride." – Maddie, book blogger

"Is it friends to lovers? Women's lit? Humorous romance? A sports romance? In the end, it's a little bit of everything." – Cat, book review

"This is a well written emotional roller coaster, which is a friends / lover's sports romance, with angst, friendships, secrets, truths, drama, twists and turns, revelations, and love, which leads to an entertaining and compelling page turner. I look forward to reading more from this talented author whose work I highly recommend." - Wendy, book review

"I would definitely pick up another book or two by this author." – Reading In the Red Room, book blogger

Content/Trigger Warnings (may contain plot spoilers)

Warning:

This book will contain explicit language, violence, and sexy times. It also has a a stalker, a dead cat, and a character who has cancer. If these are triggering for you – here is your warning to maybe avoid this book. Regardless, I promise there will be an HEA.

This book was a work of my imagination, but I did consult with professionals when writing. Any mistakes are my own and a big thank you to the medical professionals, cancer thrivers, editors, proofreaders, and others who helped me craft this story.